Stealing from the Dead

A Jack Cadance Mystery

Table of Contents

I was in a foul mood when I awoke. My mouth was dry, and I had the beginning of a minor headache. I rolled over and kissed my wife on the back of her neck. I climbed out of bed thinking of how much I wished I could have stayed there snuggled against her.

After a quick shower and shave, I went downstairs for coffee and breakfast. The bagel that remained in the bread hopper was cinnamon raisin, but I took it anyway and popped it into the toaster. I prefer butter on bagels, but it seemed we were out. A thorough search of the fridge left me in an even worse state of mind.

There was a small amount of cream cheese left, so I smeared it across the toasted surface while I frowned. The coffee was ready. I sat silently thinking about pretty much nothing.

I found the bottle of aspirin and downed a couple with a large swig of slightly too hot coffee, which caused my throat to contract. I did manage to get the pills down.

I hoped that by the time Janis got there I would be free of the headache and could get to work without the nagging of it ruining my day any further.

I heard my wife get into the shower and the kids were starting to stumble around. I smiled despite the pain, which was fading. I was a reasonably happy man who lived a reasonably decent life. My family lived in the light, in the daytime. I tried to stay with them, but my work often took me to dark places.

The metaphor was a common one for cops. I'm assigned to the Special Investigation Division of the Major Crime Unit. Janis and I investigate crimes that involve magic. We had done burglaries and extortion cases, as well as the occasional murder. She was the caster in the team. I was the normal. Well, normal is a relative word.

When I was young, I had been tested as most magically sensitive children are. It was determined I cannot use magic, but unlike most non-casters, I can sense it. Magic is everywhere, and I feel it all the time. Sometimes I feel like I have a minor headache waiting to explode into a full-blown migraine.

Sometimes I just, sort of, 'taste' magic. Recently I'd begun to learn to feel tiny differences in ambient magic. I believe it is due to higher exposure to specific spells.

I've even begun to know the difference between ambient magical energy and formatted spells from different individuals.

For me, like I said, it is like the sense of taste. Different kinds of magic have different textures and flavors. Some sweet, and others bitter. Some rough and others smooth. I'm working on being better at figuring out which is evil magic, and which is benign. Still, this unique gift had proven useful on occasion.

The official slang term for someone like me is "dud". Though I never really cared about what others say, I have heard people use the term as an insult. And often directed at me. It seems accurate though and I have decided to defuse the impact by accepting the fact that the term applies. It does rankle me sometimes though.

Since magic issues from power centers called fissures at specific locations around the world, there is always some amount of undirected magical energy permeating the world. My limitation, and if I am honest my blessing, is that I'm not an actual caster. I cannot format the power of magic into a desired spell.

I heard a loud hissing sound accompanied by a slight squeal come from out front. I hoped it was Janis. It would be better if I left the house before my family saw that I was in a bad mood again. I rose and opened the curtain enough to see that it was in fact her.

She drove an expensive flit which had all the modern conveniences. The silver and chrome surround, and high curving black shapes, were the staple of the modern design aesthetic. Four tiny headlights in a row across the front seemed to vanish in the brow shaped arc of the front hood.

Her car had a large interior and could seat seven. The tank and pistons were housed in the back and under the floor. The steam tank was powered by magic which allowed it to warm up in only a minute or so. My older standard version usually took as much as ten minutes to warm up.

I waved and motioned I would be right out.

After grabbing my hat and revolver, I slipped on my shoes and headed out the door, ignoring my wife who had just started down the stairs.

Maybe she would be mad. I was sorry for that. Still, I felt better getting away before I could take my mood out on her. I thought I heard her say something as I closed the door behind me. It was probably, “have a good day,” or, “I love you,” maybe both.

I slid into the plush leather seat next to Janis and smiled. She simply nodded. “Good morning,” I said.

She didn’t say anything for a while. As we drove down the hill toward the highway, I could tell she was also feeling tense about something. I decided to risk the question.

“What’s up?”

“Another murder,” she said casually. The tone told me she thought it was anything but another murder.

“And?” I pressed.

"It's on us. Magical. Spells were pretty standard combat stuff. So, I've been told. We'll head to the scene straight away."

"Something in your voice tells me you have more to say to me."

"Combat spells are very particular. Most casters know one or two, but this almost looked like a duel. So, I've been told. At any rate, the Guild of Aresinia is secretive and exclusive. It is the most elitist guild there is. They don't take kindly to others prying into their affairs." She kept using the phrase "so, I've been told". I bothered me a little.

"Is the guild sending investigators as well? We can work with them. If we have too, we can let them think they are the lead, and we just follow them around."

"I knew you would understand. It might not come to that, but I'm confident they will send someone. I'm just hoping they let it go so that we can just do our jobs. Still, I'd warn you to keep quiet around them, if I didn't know you knew that already."

Yeah, I knew that already. I'd had enough dealing with the guilds to know that a dud like me was worse that a normal person. Usually, they saw me as a kind of retarded or deformed thing with no actual place in either magical or normal society. That might actually be true. It didn't improve my mood.

Janis and I had a strong partnership. To say we liked each other might be a stretch. She often insulted me, and I found her arrogance difficult to stomach sometimes, but we made a good team. We'd been partners for several years now and our record was stellar minus a few minor issues. In our line of work things were bound to happen.

I know I'd made a few mistakes. Janis had as well. It was an unspoken thing that we never talked about. When we got together, we talked about our jobs.

I'd only learned about her personal life in a very peripheral way. I knew she was one of the higher-ranking members of the investigators and magical police guild known as the Chavezens. I knew, also, that she had graduated at the top of her class at University.

I always counted myself lucky that she ended up as my partner. I also was very aware that there was a reason she asked for me personally. I did not know what it might have been though.

I got the impression from how she acted that she'd been married or in a serious relationship in the past. She never talked about that either, but I knew she was single now. I'd been to her apartment, and it was as implacable as she was.

She kept it immaculately clean. Bookshelves lined almost every available wall. The furniture was all-natural woods and stone. I felt a weird sense of comfort when I was there. I wondered if that was the strong flavor of warm sweet magic which emanated from everything.

When I concentrated, I felt that same taste emanate from her. What was funny to me was the bitterness of her personality compared to how she felt to me. I suppose it might have been like magical cologne. I wondered about that and decided to ask her sometime. The time had not come so far, and I realized she would never tell me anyway. I knew she preferred to remain a mystery to me.

On the other hand, she knew everything about me. She even helped me pick out birthday presents for my family. She was genial, and almost charming, when my family was around. I found the dichotomy disturbing.

But I relished the partnership. We had both already proved many times we would do anything for the other. We'd saved each other's lives and careers more than once.

I've said before that we made an unusual team. We really didn't get together out of the office, or engage in any social events, other than those required by our work. Strictly business and strictly respectful. It had been a long time since I felt as though she thought of me as an annoyance.

When we were first teamed up, she would often offer me insults and slights. I thought then that she would have liked another partner. I was surprised to learn later that she specifically requested me.

The nagging thought was that it was so she could seem superior to me. As time went on, I discovered her reasons were related to the fact that I was a dud. She realized that my somewhat limited ability to feel magic would be an asset.

It had proved useful. Over time, I'd learned to be more discerning about the senses I felt. I could feel the difference between types of magic and even sometimes tell the difference between two peoples spells. Every bit of magic had its own flavor and color and texture. I was still learning what each was like, but I was getting better.

Janis had informed me that the murder had occurred in the tunnels under the city streets.

Seattle was a city that had literally been built on its own bones. Large sections were riddled with passages and tunnels, which had at one time been the first floors and basements of the buildings. Streets were covered over, which created interconnecting passages. These later became the dens of smugglers, fences, and other people who lived in the darkness. The maze had become known as the underground, both due to its location, and the nature of those that used it.

Over time, many of these underground lairs had been cleaned out. There were still many miles of hiding places undiscovered.

The body of the victim had been discovered near one of the known entrances in Pioneer Square. An older building, which dated from late last century, provided a large double doored access to one of the main thoroughfares, which were currently being used as an unofficial marketplace.

Here, a person could purchase pretty much anything either legal or illegal. The market was allowed to exist because it also offered refuge for some of the homeless of the city who used the market as a way of selling things that they had either found, stole, or recovered from trash bins. This offered them both employment of a sort, and a place to live.

There were also dozens of sellers who crafted items like chessboards, and jewelry from scraps. If you asked the right questions, you could also find contraband magical items, and illicit drugs from as far afield as Asia.

By the time we arrived, the Marketplace entrance had been cordoned off, and a crowd had gathered to spectate and speculate on what might have happened.

We parked near the bottom of the square on First Street and walked the half block. A uniformed sergeant, who recognized us, let us through without asking for ID.

If I had been in a better mood, I'd have let him off, but I felt I should chastise him for the lax.

"Do you know who I am?" I asked sharply. Before he could answer, I scolded him. "On a crime scene you had better ask for badges even if you recognize the person. Procedure."

"Sir," he said as he passed us through. He still didn't ask for badges.

"Whatever," I said under my breath.

"Are you okay?" Janis asked.

"Yeah, just a little headache."

We continued quietly.

After climbing down the steep stairs, we stepped through the double doors.

The large space had been cleared of people. Tables and stalls had been set up along the walls, and in a jagged line down the middle. The old concrete floor was cracked in places and stained from years of abuse. The structure of the building above was exposed and covered in stringy cobwebs and dust.

Several passages led off into the underground. We were guided to a passage heading north. This went deeper into the hillside which made up the downtown area of our city.

Less than ten yards along the gathering of uniforms indicated the location of the victim's body. My first worry was contamination of the murder site by the large contingent of people.

As Janis began her initial passes at a spell, I ordered everyone but the actual scene investigation team to disperse and secure both ends of the passage against interlopers.

The remaining cops were Janis, me, and two scene processors from the evidence team.

One of them was a medical examiner, and the other was there to collect and catalogue whatever clues Janis and I might find.

My sense of magic tingled. The magic in the area was filled with fear. The spells that had been employed left the salty flavor of terror mixed with a bitter sandpaper texture. It reminded me of the smell of bile. I had a temporary need to retch but choked it back.

I've had that kind of reaction to magic before. The overwhelming feeling surprised me. Also, it made me think that whatever magic had been used was both powerful and ancient.

The body was wrapped in clear plastic. The rigid form looked for all the world like some modern mummy. The work had been carefully done. My first thought was that the murderer was a highly organized or obsessive person.

The murder had occurred somewhere else, and the body had been left here.

If for disposal, it was a bad location. Hundreds, if not thousands, of people might come by it at any time. Indeed, it seemed to have been left there only the night before and had been discovered as the market began business in the early hours.

The body radiated the magic, which I had sensed when I focused on it. Whatever had happened, it was a deep magic which only powerful casters might be able to perform. That only narrowed the field of suspects to maybe a thousand in the general Seattle area.

The stone and concrete floor and walls left no other clues. Our course of investigation would be left with whatever witnesses we might find and the body itself. The uniforms had been interviewing people for possible clues, and the Examiner team would be transporting the body to the coroner's office as soon as we released it.

I left Janis to continue her part of the investigation and joined in with the witness questioning.

One of the officers pointed me to the three kids who had discovered the body. They stood off to one side leaning against a brick partition.

As I approached, they stood away from the wall and stepped toward me. The oldest of them was a boy of maybe 15. The other two were younger girls and might have been twins. They all wore somewhat bedraggled clothing and had shoes which seemed both ill-fitting and at the end of their life.

Poverty and homelessness had always been a problem in the city. Generation upon generation of underemployed or illegally employed persons and their families slept in tents and under the city streets.

It was further evidence of the very stratified class system which had always plagued Seattle. Elite business and magical concerns held both wealth and power. The stratified organization of workers below them left very little room for elevating oneself from his station at birth.

It cost either money or exceptional talent to move up. Most of the time it would require both. The only place there was any exception to the rule was if you were born with magical ability. Depending on the nature and power of your abilities, you could either raise to great heights or fall off the map.

In my case, I simply stayed at roughly the same level as my parents. My sister had developed into something of an exceptional corporate mage, and I was proud she had managed to rise from our humble station.

The kids waited patiently as I approached. They seemed timid and nervous as though they were under some suspicion. It made me think that their regular means of life was perhaps less than legal.

I wasn't there to confront them and wanted to reassure them that they could speak freely.

"Hello," I said. "I understand you three found the body back there," I thumbed toward the passage.

"Yeah," the boy replied. "We were just minding our own business coming to the market to pick up some stuff when we tripped over it. That's all,"

"Were any of you hurt?" I asked trying to clear the air.

"No," one of the girls said. She looked down at the floor quickly as though she might not be telling me the truth.

"If you are hurt, I can get a doctor to look at it," I replied.

"I don't trust no doctors," she said quietly. "The last one took us away from mom and said she had to stop drinking the stuff before he'd give us back,"

I realized she was talking about a social worker who must have been a doctor and reassured her that it would not happen again.

"No worries, what are your names?" I asked.

"I'm Bill, that's my sister Jessie, and our friend Martha,"

"Here then," I continued. "Tell me about how you found the dead body,"

"I tripped over it. It was just lying there in the dark and we know the passages. When I tripped it glowed bright for a second and made it hard to see. Then it went dark again. Bill pulled out his lighter and sparked it up and we saw it was a dead person. We know there is a reward for finding a body. Bill called the cops to collect,”

“That’s true,” I said smiling. “Fifty bucks is a lot of money. What do you plan on doing with it?”

“I’m going to buy some new shoes and some candy,” said the other girl smiling.

“My business,” Bill said. “As long as I don’t do nothing illegal, I can spend my money the way I want,”

“That’s true,” I replied. It was then that I sensed it. The boys texture. Like salted pork and wire bristles. He had a strong aura of magic. It was not a spell or anything like that. It was more the sense that he was steeped in the same magical aura which I sometimes felt from strong casters.

Being homeless and probably not in school, it was possible that he’d managed to slip under the radar of the system which was designed to identify and educate young potential mages.

His aura was strong enough that I doubted he’d gone unnoticed by everyone. There was also the chance he'd been recruited by a non-guild group known as The Underground. These outcasts believed that the guild system was unnatural and limited a casters ability. By not belonging to a guild, he could fully explore his abilities.

It occurred to me for a moment that here in the underground we were likely to find members of The Underground. My headache faded a little and I smiled at the irony. If Janis felt his innate ability, she'd do her best to get him in an apprenticeship at one of the guild schools.

For myself I didn't care one way or another. My first thought was to find whatever clues I could to help solve a murder. Telling Janis about the kid would be a side task which I'd get around too when I felt that it was correct to do so.

"You kids come down here often, right? Did you notice anyone hanging around that you haven't seen before? Someone who didn't look like they fit in?" I asked.

“Not this morning,” One of the younger kids said shyly. “Last night there was an old rich guy who came down to buy some Blends,”

Blends were a sort of magical narcotic concoction, which offered a very euphoric effect and were highly addictive. They’d been illegal for decades and as something which crossed the line between the mundane and the magical, Janis and I had been involved in a few Blend busts. Most of the perps had been un-guilded casters, and back room chemists, working together to make a small drug empire for themselves. One of the larger busts involved resources from cities all over the west coast and resulted in more than one hundred arrests from Seattle to Los Angeles.

If the rich man were really rich, he’d have a better source of the drugs than the underground market. My initial thought was the man simply looked more well off then these kids, which, in their eyes, made him rich.

It might be worth checking into, but I doubted he was our man.

“Did you see anyone from one of the guilds?”

“Guilds don’t come down here,” the older boy said. His voice seemed fearful, and I could tell that he had some natural distrust of the formal system. This gave weight to my first thought about him being trained by the underground.

“I see,” I said wanting to put him at ease. “Probably nothing then. I’ll need to know how to get ahold of you to get you your reward. I don’t need an actual address, only your names and where I can find you when I need too,”

“We already told you our names. And you can find us here most mornings. We do the pickup for Mom,” Bill said in a snarky tone.

“Ok. It will take a few days to check everything out,” I said. “Once that has been done, I’ll personally come back with the cash. Sound good?”

“What do you mean check everything out? Why can’t you just give us the money now?” Martha interjected. It was the first time she’d spoken, and I was startled by her raspy and yet high-pitched voice. She sounded like a mouse with tuberculosis.

“Oh, you know, paperwork needs doing, and all that. I don’t like it either. Procedures and rules and all that. It’s a real pain in the keester. But I’m a cop. I gotta’ follow the rules. I promise I’ll see too it myself.”

“You best,” Bill said.

I smiled. Despite the rough around the edges attitude, I found that I quite liked the kid. I hoped that maybe he could get organized into a guild and elevate his place in the world. As it was, he was living in the shadows, on the fringe of society. A sponsor or an apprenticeship meant money and social standing. He could bring real change to those he loved.

After I got the information from the kids, I rejoined Janis. She was standing near the body looking down one of the off-branching tunnels.

“Find something?” I asked.

“There is a faint trail of residual magic going off down that way. Though it is fading, I think we can follow it for maybe another hour before it fades completely.”

I called over the examiner and told him to finish up at the site. I also informed him we’d be checking out a few clues in the underground, and to be prepared with his team should we call.

Janis led the way so that I would not confuse the trail. By staying a few paces behind her, my aura would not disrupt the residual magic. Because it was fading quickly, any interaction might ruin her ability to follow. She held a small lantern before her, which she’d procured from the uniforms to illuminate the tunnel ahead.

I could sense she had an active spell. It felt like cloves and honey, the smell of a sweet bread baking in the oven. Her spells always made me feel comfortable. Even the few combat spells I'd seen her cast had a sort of warm and inviting feel to me. I knew that it was because I trusted her. Similar spells I'd felt from others had a harsh acid taste.

Although the tunnels followed a roughly rectangular pattern, they oftentimes cut across at the angle of a destroyed foundation, or where new passages were cut into the hillside. We crossed and re-crossed several larger main passages as we wound our way deeper into the underground. It was more than thirty minutes before we came to the end of the trail.

The room we were in was probably a basement of one of the older buildings further up the hill from the square. One wall was partially caved in. The other three walls formed a large space of perhaps fifty feet to a side. Pillars of stacked and mortared stone served as supports from the building above.

In the center of the room stood a large pedestal. It was about seven feet to a side and maybe thirty inches high. I felt the magic which emanated from its upper surface. The bad sour taste was nearly unpalatable. I shied away as we entered the chamber. Janis sensed my apprehension and paused to prepare a defensive spell. Her action clouded out the bad feeling, and I felt more comfortable entering the room.

I could feel the power of the spell. I had no idea what its effect would have been. Janis could determine the actual spell used, provided the caster had been trained in any of the guilds. There were standard formulae that were traceable based on principles of casting. Each guild had its own system of building spells. Once a caster understood how each guild formatted its magic, it could be relatively easy to trace the spell. Sometimes, Janis could trace it back to the caster by way of the guilds records of members who use certain formulas to construct their spells.

She pondered over the dais for several minutes while I wandered the chamber looking for anything that might be important.

Low levels of light filtered down through pink and green glass. These were inset into the concrete and made up the parts of sidewalk above. The eerie illumination made the entire area seem haunted.

I paced each wall and noted the locations of four other passages leading off into the underground. Only the one we had entered seemed to have been used recently. No other tracks, except ours, marked the dusty stones of the floor.

I paced a grid across the room starting on what I assumed was the north wall. Back and forth I paced, slowly looking at the floor, the ceiling, and at any features which seemed likely to offer a clue.

The overhead of the exposed structure offered very little in the way of information. The brickwork of the walls showed that one of them had been added later, possibly as a way of partitioning off a larger space. These were heavy grey cinder blocks as opposed to the smaller red traditional brick. It was the floor that caught my attention. Traced in intricate patterns, I could make out symbols carved into the old cement flooring.

Long curves and weaving lines were etched creating a sort of maze, or pattern in the room. The dais marked the center of the maze.

"Janis," I paused. "You should see this."

She stopped the chant and turned toward me. Her shoulders shrugged as if to ask what it was that I had seen.

"The floor," I nodded, indicating the pattern.

"We must start at the beginning then," she said in a soft yet strong voice.

As she crossed the room, she examined the maze and turned toward one corner. I followed closely, and once there she stood erect and began another chant. This spell had the same honey and cinnamon flavor with an aftertaste of candied raisons.

The floor began to glow. Lines of magical force flowed from where we stood, toward the first opening along the outer section on the pattern.

She stepped toward the opening. I saw the floor light up at each step. She stepped in time with the pulsing light and the chant. I was unsure if the light followed her chant, or the chant followed the pulsing of the light. I marched behind her in sync with both.

At first, it felt as though the entire floor lit up at her steps, but I realized as we proceeded through the maze, that each step started a fast wave of light from where she placed her feet toward the edges of the room. Each flash seemed to be like a heartbeat.

My heart was in fact beating in time with our footfalls, and her chanting, and the pulses. Thum-a-thump, thum-a-thump. We made a turn in the maze to the left and began to arc along a stretch, which looked like it would cross a section of the collapsed wall.

Janis added something to her chant. The bricks cleared a path for us as though they had a life of their own. In moments, the entire wall returned to pristine condition. The floor beneath was swept clean of both dust and debris by her spell.

Her chant returned to what it had been before. She hadn't missed a step, but it seemed to me that she was straining in some way. Though I could not see her face, I could tell from the flavor of the spell that she was starting to sweat. Her spell now carried a salty undertone, which almost offset the cloying sweetness which normally accompanied her magic.

For my part, I also felt as though I were carrying some burden. At first, it was light but at each step I felt somehow heavier, as though I added a pound a beat. Thum-a-thump, Thum-a-thump, Thum-a-thump, if this didn't let up soon, I'd be unable to move. I estimated the number of steps remaining, and thought, at best, it might be one hundred and fifty. Already, I was straining under the magical weight of proceeding.

Another small change to the chant made me feel a little stronger, or less week maybe. The weight didn't abate, but I felt I could bear it better. Still, my knees and shoulders were aching. Thum-a-thump, Thum-a-thump, Thum-a-thump.

After several turns, we found ourselves facing the final few feet near the center of the maze. From here, we only needed to pass around to the other side of the dais, and we would be in the center.

The final steps were agony. The last turn seemed to open up before us. While in the maze, there didn't seem to be anything on the dais, but now that we looked down the final few feet, it looked as though a body was laying peacefully upon it.

The sensation was not unlike walking down a long hall. At first, I could only make out the body, as I got closer, I could see that the entire room was different than it had appeared to be.

Ahead, I could make out lines of magical force which extended through out the room in intricate patterns. The room seemed to have a ceiling made of hammer metal square with circles in the center, and the shape of arcane symbols in relief. The walls were painted with scenes representing some sort of forest gathering.

The end of the room which had been walled off with cinder blocks, stood open to the world and exposed a glade of trees and grass overlooking a body of water, which looked as though it might be Puget Sound. We stepped into the center of the maze and into another world.

Upon the pedestal lay a dozen bouquet of flowers in a splash of color and fragrance. The sunlight shone through the open wall illuminating the room in such brightness that I could see clouds of pollen refract a rainbow of colors. My eyes almost hurt from the glare.

Janis strode directly toward the alter and knelt at the side sliding her hands across the surface as though she were tracing the elegant arcane symbols engraved in rugged rows on all its surfaces.

I walked toward the center of the room amazed at the vision. I assumed it to be a kind of illusion. I could taste a myriad of flavors of magic, as though the whole scene was some sort of construct of spells from a dozen sources.

I had heard of group spells. When many casters got together and performed highly intricate and very powerful magic, they could share the burden of casting. I had never witnessed the results though. It was incredibly difficult to get more than one person to follow the highly specific formula, which were required for a spell of that complexity.

Janis told me long ago that casting was a very personal thing. Spells were like voices. You might sing the same notes, but the actual timber and vibrato of the individual singer were unique. I once heard it related using a painter's metaphor as well. Brush strokes being different for every individual artist.

In any case, the effect was that no two casters were exactly identical, and as a result no two spells had exactly the same effect, even when constructed the same. There was even a study of the great casters of the past and how over time their spells, which were otherwise the same, changed as they became more skilled.

The upshot was that it was difficult to get two or more people involved in casting a spell. From my understanding, it could take years for people to attune to each other enough to make something like that work.

Here though, was a very complex casting, which even I could tell had been done collaboratively. I could sense at least seven different textures to the spell and a few flavors which seemed to be some combination of the individual components.

As I let my feelings flow, I could tell that each spell had been cast upon one of the seven cardinal symbols, which were engraved at equidistant points around the alter.

Something about the number seven began to ring in my memory. Although I hadn't really thought about it, I seemed to remember that there were seven major casting guilds. There were a dozen smaller, more specialized guilds. These had come into being in the last few centuries. If I wasn't mistaken, there had been seven originally.

Each had some level of crossover of one or more of the others, but in General. They all played very specific roles in society for managing the use and education of the respective members of each guild. The Magista was a guiding authority over all the guilds.

Aresinia is a military guild. The crossed sword and shield symbol on the floor glowed a dull red and gold. Most countries employed this guild in some fashion for national defense. The rarest of the casters were the combat mages and they dealt with battle magic. Fireballs and exploding arrows were their stock in trade. They could also create large scale defenses to ward off battle mages most devastating attacks. Since magic was outlawed for actual warfare, they generally acted as military advisors, and as a sort of deterrent.

The Talismantecha was organized to provide magically enhanced technology. Vehicles and home appliances were the most visible results of their craft. They oversaw spells which were infused into material objects and thus usable by anyone. Their hammer and square symbol shone in silver and orange.

The Chavezen inspectors guild of police was exactly what it sounded like. Blue and white light emanated from the seven-pointed star of their guild. Janis was a high-ranking member of that guild. I learned from her that the guild name came from its founder Rumira Chavez, who was said to be the first to use spells to solve crimes. She set up the basic format of criminal investigation, as well as the rules for justly using spells. This was referred to as the Chavezen Code. It was often sited in court when someone thought they had had their rights violated.

The medical guild was called Children of Hermes. They developed healing magics and created elixirs to combat variety of ailments. They also oversaw research into longevity and other health related spells. A red and white caduceus was their symbol.

Via De Naturnal were both horticulturists as well as astrologers. A green tree and silver star traced lines of text on the floor. Most of their efforts were in reading signs and portends and understanding how the natural world works. Many of their spells utilized magic which revolved around the cycle of life and death. They were often thought of as being somewhat aloof and perhaps mentally flighty. I had heard it said that they could tell you your future, but only in a riddle.

Elementarae had originally been called the philosophers guild. They formed a unique guild which practiced magics formulated from only elemental components. They were one of the few houses that crossed the lines between all of the systems and created a number of battle, healing and natural spells. They also used flame divination which was similar to the technique used by Via De

Naturnal. I often thought of them as generalists who focused not of the result of their spells but on the construct based on the four elements. Red, brown, blue and white quartered a circle with a leaf, a snowflake, a wave, and a brazier.

The final guild was one that had not been active in centuries. The Necromages dealt with death. To hear it from their supporters, that also meant life. It was said they used to have healing magics but worked almost exclusively with death. By reanimating or inspecting a corpse they could tell the future or the past. In the old days, armies of the fallen had waged war. The unsavory nature of the guild had slowly led to its decline. It was said there were fewer than twenty left in the entire world. Their symbol of a skull traced in black and white glowed very faintly.

It was also true that most guilds had smaller specialized colleges. These focused on even more specific features of functions of the guilds primary calling. The Talismantecha, for instance, had colleges for household items, another for vehicles, and others to oversee very specific items for a variety of uses.

I understood those from recent experience, and I knew of the colleges for Chavezen forms, due to my own career interests. The truth was that no one really understood the guilds but their own leading members.

I followed a line of light as it passed along the floor from the elemental symbol toward the Dais. Several symbols created an arc of writing that wound from the right to the left in a single spiral arm ending just where Janis was kneeling.

I looked at the flowers on the alter and realized they had been formed into the shape of a human body. I also saw that each limb was constructed of flowers which represented the colors of the guilds.

The right arm was Talismantecha, the left Elementarea. The legs were made up of the Via De Naturnal and the Aresinia. The head represented the Chavezen. The upper body seemed to be red and white of the Children of Hermes, and the lower body black and white of the Necromages.

I was remined of a story I'd heard in my youth of a man who sees a vision of a statue. When he goes to the head of the Via De Naturnal for an interpretation, he is told that the world is formed the same as a person. Each part of the whole, and each lending skill and purpose to his being.

The right hand is to do. The left hand is to strive toward. The left foot is where you stand, and the right where you travel. The head is the guide, and the heart is the will. The liver is where your challenges are purified.

In retrospect, I think I was feeling a little philosophical at that moment, but standing in the middle of an illusion of such power might have that effect on a person. My mind was trying to comprehend something that only those who could use magic could understand. By giving it an allegory, I was allowing myself to hold on to something which grounded it in my mind. Had I not done this, I might have been driven mad by the experience. My personal history with magical crime had taught me many ways of dealing with those things which I cannot understand.

Janis stood up and slowly walked toward me. The way she held her hands toward me made me think she was trying to warn me about something. When she got within an arms-reach she took me by the shoulder and turned me around pushing me toward the exit.

We walked back along the path of the maze slowly, almost tiptoeing. There was a nervous apprehension from her that said we were in trouble.

She sensed my concern and pressed her finger to her lips to keep me from asking. Turn after turn we retraced our steps. Finally, we stepped back into the passage from which we had come.

“We are in trouble,” she said in a quiet voice. “You and I have just traversed to a place where we should not go. Now we only have a short time to remove the effect of the place or die.”

“Die?” I gasped. A small cough escaped my lips.

“That place is flooded with magic from a thousand years of spells being built up, one on top of the next. It forms a sort of clock. We are now intrinsically attached to the clock. The clock chimes at noon. That is only four hours and six minutes from now. We have to get the spells purged from us or we will die when the effect of the spell goes off."

"You mean the spell is there to kill us. Like a trap or something?" I asked.

"No, the effect of the spell is much broader and more subtle. There is so much magic poured into the spell that we will be consumed when it goes off," she sighed. "The spell itself is a sort of alarm clock which has been running perpetually for millennia. I don't know its whole function, but it is very, very powerful. By navigating the maze, we unwittingly became part of the mechanics of the spell. We may even have altered the way the spell was meant to function."

"How do we get rid of the spell?" I asked.

Janis riffled through her pocket and produced a small hourglass shaped object. She closed her eyes and tapped the top of it four times then handed it to me.

"Here is your timer," she smiled. "If we don't get it done by the time it goes off, we'll both be dead." She seemed to be holding back something.

"Okay," I repeated. "How do we get rid of this spell?"

"There are a number of ways. The first and easiest is to get to a magical healer and have them siphon off the residual energy. It will leave us both unable to use or sense magic for some time, but should suffice to keep us alive,"

"Let's go then," I turned to retrace our steps.

"Wait," she stopped me. "Not just any healer can do this. We need someone with experience in dueling magic."

"But in General, dueling is against the law. Who would have that kind of skill?"

"You're right, it's not legal, but it still happens all the time," she sighed. "Not to worry, I know someone, but..."

"But?"

"You must never tell anyone about it. It is a bit of an embarrassment. My ex-husband is a Duel master."

I was flabbergasted. She told me something about her past without me needing to pry it from her. Secondly, that she would have associated with someone who operated outside the law. Third, that she had been married.

I knew her devotion to the Guilds was solid, but she had been a cop for more than a decade. Her loyalty to the rule of law was higher than anything, and I couldn't imagine her acting or interacting with anyone who might compromise that.

"Why dueling?" I asked.

"That place is a dueling den. It exists outside the real world and therefore is beyond the normal rule of law. Those who hold to the old traditions use places like that to engage in the activity, which would otherwise be illegal. It must have been created by a joint spell from a member from each of the primary guilds. The duels might not actually occur there."

“Just to have a place to duel?” I was shocked that so much effort would go into something which on the surface seemed so trivial.

“Not exactly. In the old days, troubles and vendetta would be solved in duels. They would happen once every few years at a specific time. All the interested parties would gather at the dueling location and announce their intention to participate. The practice was also used to determine the ruling guild for the next few years. Once the time of the duel had past, then the location would close, and no more challenges could be issued until the next time it opened. The duels needn’t occur in the den.”

“So, this location closes in four hours?” I asked.

“Yes. We will die unless the spell is abated.”

“Seems a little harsh.” I opined.

“Yes, it is.”

It had taken us more than an hour to find the dueling den. Although we could move quicker retracing our steps, I was worried that with so little time left we might not get to someone who could dissipate the energy from the spell, and therefore we would die a horrible death.

I could only assume it would be horrible. I suppose that any death by such means would be considered horrible. And, as yet, I was quite unprepared to leave what I considered to be a good life.

Janis made a spell which would allow us to find the location again. Another ten minutes of wasted time. Finally, we began to wind our way back through the tunnels. We talked as we went.

“Leaving the body of the defeated in that passage was no accident,” I said. “They were meant to be found. As a warning, do you think?”

“It seems likely,” she nodded. “I suppose that this dueling group has some larger purpose than simply to fight it out to the death. Perhaps there is a motive which drives them to duel," she pondered. "If I were to guess, I'd say that this was not the last death. A warning to others who were drawn to the duels for whatever purpose. The winner has said, beware."

"So, once we get ourselves free of the spell our challenge will be to discover the reason for them to duel," I mused.

"No, our first purpose is to discover the other members of the group who might be dueling. Identifying the body and stopping any future duel must come first. We only have a short time, and before that time is expired, we can remove the spell,"

"Do you mean to say we must carry this curse with us till the end? What if we don't make it in time?"

"Yes. It will take time to treat the spell. Time, which we don't have. This is a race against the clock. I believe that the real purpose for the duels is more sinister than you might imagine," she sighed. I was beginning to hate it when she sighed.

“Consider this,” she went on, “In the dueling room there are symbols from each of the major guilds. With one dead already it might be that there will potentially be another five who will die. Five in four hours,” she said.

“Why not simply wait at the chamber till the next duelers come forward?” I asked.

“If I am not mistaken, we have another problem,” I didn’t like what she was implying.

“The Duel did not occur in that chamber. That was the place where those who were part of the challenge went to announce their intention to be part of the duels. By walking the maze, we inadvertently announced we are part of the competition. We are therefore marked. Anyone else who has gone through the ritual will be able to locate us and challenge us to the duel. A geas is now placed on us. We must fight to live or remove the geas. And if I’m not mistaken there can be only one survivor for this particular quest.”

“But the spell can be taken off us, right?”

“I think the power which it has over us may be siphoned off so that we may only fall sick for a short time after. I’m not sure we can completely remove ourselves from the effect without engaging in the duel itself," again she sighed.

"You are in a very precarious position though. The combats are designed to be magical in nature. As a non-caster," she used that term instead of 'Dud'. "You will be unable to defend yourself."

"As for me, I have done very little dueling. My combat spells will probably serve me well, but those who have purposefully put themselves forward will have practiced and prepared, making them formidable opponents. Under the best of conditions, I would say we, either of us, have little chance should it come to dueling."

"Then we will have to cheat," I said.

"Well, I had thought of that. I might have a way of helping you should it come to it, but I'm afraid the nature of the duels will be one on one. No direct interference will be allowed. Whatever help I offer must come before any potential combat takes place. This, by way of preparing you."

"Okay?" my question was implied.

"I have an idea about your magical senses. Also, I may be able to locate enchanted items which will help you."

We'd seen this type of item before. Magically infused objects were available for thousands of normal daily chores and uses. We had even come across some underground items, which allowed normal people to cast very potent spells, even some defensive and offensive combat spells. Objects such as that would naturally be illegal.

As much as I did not like the idea, I knew that I would not stand a chance otherwise.

"Okay, where do we go?"

"The evidence lockup has dozens of magically enhanced eggs from a case we worked on recently. We will check them out and I'll show you how to use some of them. Might be, we can give you a fighting chance."

"Thanks," I smiled. "Seems like we might have just done ourselves in."

"We aren't beaten yet," she said in a firm voice.

Once back at the market, we checked in with the scene processing team. The body had been taken to the morgue and identified. Several boxes of potential clues were available for us to go through which were back at the station in our office.

Janis drove us to the morgue first so that we could validate the identity of the deceased.

It was only a half mile to the morgue, but we drove it anyway knowing that time was at a premium. What would have taken ten minutes of walking took only three minutes to drive. After parking in the main underground lot, we crossed to the morgue.

The examiner had not processed the body yet. It lay on the slab of a stainless-steel table. A white sheet was draped over it with only a long toe tag dangling from one end.

We checked in quickly then began our examination. Janis left off using any spells as the time required would count against our clock.

The man was a member of the Children of Hermes guild. His name was Johnathon Albertage. Although a prominent physician, he was otherwise not highly placed in the organization. He specialized in family medicine at a clinic in West Seattle.

Initially, this left us with feeling we were missing something. The coroner confirmed he had been killed when his heart was stopped with a combat spell which was reasonably difficult to produce. There were other signs of violence upon him as well. Several bruises along his arm indicated some sort of restraining spell, which tightly constricted, causing contusions. Janis surmised he had been held down using one spell in order to precisely target the organs with the next spell, which had killed him.

Other abrasions indicated it had not been a quick battle. The coroner also reported residual magic, which indicated he'd cast several spells either in defense or attack.

I allowed the background noise of magic to abate somewhat so I could sense the aura surrounding the victim. Perhaps I could get a feeling for the one who had done this to him. The taste was all pepper and rot. I quickly tongued my lips to wipe away the imagined flavor, and allowed the white wash of magic to disguise the unwanted sensation.

A hunch was beginning to play along the back of my mind. Now that we knew who this person was, I thought his identity might be the key to solving the mystery. I also felt that there must be more to the murder than simply some crazy dueling society.

“Janis,” I interjected, “I’m going to head out to the front desk. They have a library terminal there and I have a few ideas I’d like to pursue.”

“I think we have all we can get from here anyway,” she sighed, “I’ll come with.”

We commandeered the terminal. While I operated it, Janis sat just behind me and watched over my shoulder.

I started with a simple search of the victim. He had earned various minor awards. Articles written by him indicated he was something of an expert on early magical development in children. His family had been in the medical profession for generations going back to The Reckoning.

The Reckoning happened in the early eighteenth century. Over a period of twenty years, various laws were instituted to outlaw prosecution of casters. A resultant counter from magic users, was they instituted rules prohibiting use of magic against normal. This détente initiated the beginnings of the modern collaboration between the divergent peoples.

It had been said that it was due to an American president fathering a powerful caster. He'd been concerned over possible persecution, and started working toward reconciliation instead.

For my part, I believed that to be a made-up story. The death toll on both sides of the undeclared war had risen to apocalyptical proportions, and the only real solution was to find a tenable peace.

The general laws of magic had been instituted in almost every nation along the same lines. Though a few nations had slightly different versions, the Chavezen code ushered in a lasting, if tentative, peace.

He also belonged to a number of professional and social organizations. One in particular caught our attention.

The Order of The Path was an ancient fraternity. I suppose the word fraternity is not the correct usage, since, according to what little I knew, they had always included anyone regardless of sex, or race. The only particular requirement was all the members were casters.

It was a relatively small society bosting no more than a few thousand members in the larger Seattle area. This limited membership was probably due to the order's overarching mandate of general equality amongst all casters, regardless of their skill or power level. They believed that any spark of magic was divine no matter how small.

I knew that at least one "dud" had been a member. I was also surprised to learn that several extremely powerful magicians were also counted on their roles.

Most casters thought of them as a fringe group with somewhat heretical beliefs. Those that belonged to the order often hid their membership in order to avoid incurring distain from other casters.

The membership role of the order was not published, but there were a few people who advertised their association. These were mostly people with progressive political ideals who worked for a more even system of treatment in caster society as a whole.

Personal articles from the corpse had been catalogued and photographed for evidence. I pulled the list up on the viewer and flipped through each item, one by one, allowing both of us to examine them thoroughly.

He had a class ring from a prominent university in the east. Miskatonic University in Arkham was situated along a river of the same name in Massachusetts. It had been established in the early days of the colonization but converted to a center for magical learning after the reckoning.

As one of the premier universities, Albertage would have been afforded a certain status due to the prestige from his alma mater. His life was somewhat simple, however, and though he had been married for some years, he never fathered any children. I recorded his address and the name of his wife for reference. I supposed it would end up being Janis and I that would report his death to her.

I never liked that part of the business, but I often found it worked in our favor to be the ones who informed the family. We could learn a lot by watching how each person reacted to the news. Sometimes clues presented themselves in subtle ways. I shelved the idea for now while I continued to delve into Albertage's background.

There were dozens of articles in various medical and magical journals. Many of these were opinion pieces about the state of medical care in the country as opposed to the rest of the world. He often sited other nations for their more generous medical practices. He was especially vocal about early childhood care.

The few actual medical papers he'd written were rehashes of various treatment considerations and arguments over magical versus chemical medical formulations. I could see that he was highly verbose and decently articulate. He did sometimes tend toward the over wordy. Still, I found I liked him. You can tell a lot about a person by reading things that they have written.

Why a man like him would be involved in a dueling society was beyond me. His specific skill set was hardly conducive to combat magic. He must have learned some dueling or battle spells at some point, but his oath as a Doctor should have prevented him from harming anyone.

I found myself more confused about the victim than when I'd started.

I made a list of the other organizations he belonged too and the location of his office so we could conduct interviews. A hunch told me we would not find anything more about him than I already managed from the general inquiry.

While I worked, Janis had been reviewing what we'd found on the body and sorted through the magical information she'd gathered. She had determined the spells used and informed me that our killer was likely a member of the police and security guild. The Chavezian style was very easy to detect. She had noticed it as soon as she started. She only needed a little time to determine the exact spells and power level, which could further narrow whoever might have been responsible. We had several little clues to follow now.

We had used more than 45 minutes of our remaining time, which made me wonder if I was wasting time. Somehow, we would need to move faster if we were to survive.

Janis told me she felt a resonance nearby which she thought might be the effect of the geas which had been placed on us. For my part, I did feel a certain uneasiness. A taste like brine caused an involuntary reaction. It bit the back of my throat and caused a slight gag as I concentrated on it. I found that the flavor seemed to be directional. By turning one way and the other, I found it to be either stronger or weaker.

Somewhere to the east was a magical danger, which represented either my death or my salvation.

“It’s close,” Janis told me. “Time to go.”

“I feel it too. What should I do?” I hesitated.

“We will have to act quickly,” she nodded. “No time for formalities or preparation. If we work this correctly, we can get you cleared of the threat.”

“What about you?” I asked.

“I have a plan for me. If all else fails, I intend to see this through,” she smiled.

That worried me.

She might have a card to play later, and I wondered why I should be worried. She’d faced some difficult situations before and always came through. There was always the chance she was overconfident. I knew her to be capable and she could defend herself against most, but the idea of a dueling challenge worried me.

When I relaxed my mind, I could almost see the line of force which emanated from the east. I say line, but in reality it was more of a curled and wispy film of smoke. As I said before, the brine taste was nauseating. I tasted it in irregular waves. The more I calmed my mind the easier it was to stomach the undesired sensation.

As we left the coroner's office and walked down the steps of the old gray stone building, I could feel the light rain, cold and clean, tapping against my face. I felt better and more alert. The sense of impending action caused everything to slow down for me. Time seemed to stretch.

I turned eastward up 4th Avenue. Janis walked to my left. The feeling of being drawn toward some unknown destiny was palpable. My hand ached to grip my revolver in preparation of the unknown enemy I was soon to face.

They say that a person facing an impending death sees the world more clearly. I'd read what inmates on death row had to say on the subject and found that I, too, felt a certain clarity of purpose at that moment, perhaps not of an impending death. It seemed to me to be a feeling that the future was set.

I was inexorably attracted to a single moment of time which was now within…, how many steps? It must be close. My mind cleared even further, and I realized I'd walked more than seven blocks up the hill toward the First Hill district. The direction of the gaes turned north at that point and I again followed. If I could guess, I'd probably lost another half hour of precious time.

Two more blocks brought me to a park nestled next to the construction which would someday be a large highway running through the downtown. A large set of pillars would someday support an overpass. They cast long shadows along the grassy knoll. Below I felt another spell adding to the one I was following.

The new sensation of cooked cabbage and carrots filled my mind, a sort of comfort food without any real flavor of its own. It was barren of the spices of some meat, like corned beef. I found that I quite liked the combination of the brine and the cabbage. The two flowed together and complimented each other. Each on its own would have been unpalatable.

"We are here," Janis said in a quiet voice. "I'm going to tell you a secret. You must completely believe me, or you are doomed to die horribly. Are you ready?"

"I guess so," I wasn't.

"Magic cannot actually harm you if you don't let it. To a caster magic is real and therefore has real effects. To the uninitiated it is real because of the superstition so ingrained that the weak minded will believe it. But for you, you know it has power and you are strong enough to resist. You are powerful enough to close your mind and body to the effect and let them pass over you without harming you. You must do this to survive the duel."

"I'm not sure what you mean?" I was filled with both doubt and a lack of understanding.

"Feel the magic. Feel it come toward you. Feel it flow over you and experience it not as the attack, but as a flow of sensations, which touch only your senses. Then bend the power around you and past you and let it dissipate without effect. You can contort the flow of power with your will. You are unique in your power. You may not cast a spell, but you can manipulate the energy of one that is already cast."

"How do I do that?" My apprehension grew. My voice almost cracked.

"Your senses will let you feel it. Like fear, you must control the feeling. Will the power away from you. Redirect the flow of the spell."

"I'll try."

She smiled at me as though I were a cherished child.

"I'll explain everything once you get through this. I promise," she added.

We crossed to where the man stood between the giant pillars. I could tell he'd already built up a defensive spell, and patiently waited for us to come within talking distance.

I had seen several films that featured magical duels. These grandiose affairs were glamorized as entertainment guaranteed to excite. In the theatre, there were highly stylized rules which were supposed to give a certain gentlemanly honor to the entire affair.

Because I didn't know better, I walked within twenty paces and faced the man.

He was tall and lean. His friendly face seemed both affable and genial. In another circumstance I might have called him friendly. He wore a traditional robe of the Elementarae. It was obvious his specialty was water magic.

The robe was dark blue with fine threads of white forming a raindrop pattern over the majority of the garment. At the cuffs and along the hem these threads worked a pattern of even waves running toward the center of his body. A belt of pale green was clasped by a broach rendered in an Asian floret.

He made the required semantics which indicated he was ready to face me. I simply saluted him and smiled. It was a very forced smile. I didn't feel happy or friendly in that moment. In fact, I felt a great fear which I had never known before.

I face death in one way or another regularly. In the heat of the moment, when being shot at, I usually don't feel anything. I do as I need to do to survive. So far this had served me well.

"I have come by the will of the wheel of fortune. I will face you and my fate. I duel for primacy. I fight for the right to lead," he spoke the words as though entranced.

"I face your challenge by the wheel of fortune. I embrace my fate. I duel for justice. I fight for the right to live," I'm not sure where I got the words, but they seemed to fit.

He looked at me as though amused and began an incantation. The smile reminded me of something. I realized I'd seen him before, but I could not place him in my memory. I pushed the memory to the back of my mind to focus on the needs of the moment.

I'd faced off against casters before and prevailed. Never in so forced a setting though. In every case before, it was kill or be killed with instant and sudden action resulting in no time for the mind to conceive of the horror of death, or the pain of injury. It was all action, not thought. Perhaps that wasn't entirely true, but the emotional element was rarely there.

But now I stood there feeling everything I'd never expected to feel. I felt his energy building as he prepared a spell. I tasted the energy of it. I smelled the brine of the geas. I knew the tremor of my own doubt building in me. My hands came up reflexively as if to ward off whatever power he would set at me.

I could taste the swell of power. This time it was organic and fishy. Time slowed even more as the wave of energy moved toward me. At first it was lightning speed. As it reached me the power slowed to a crawl. The air was compressed by the wave of power. A ripple of humidity danced in the space between the Elementarae and me.

I slowly reached out with a finger and touched the rainbow of light that danced along the edges of the wave. It crackled along my finger like miniature lightning.

Then it began to hurt, first along the finger then through the hand. I fought the sensation. Reflexively, I pushed it away. I yelled loudly and concentrated on the wave. I visualized the colors crashing harmlessly along a large rocky shore.

The pain subsided. An acrid odor filled my nose and mouth. Stumbling backward at the force of the wave, my world moved super-fast for a moment. In a sudden, time slowed again.

The disconnected feeling of the flow of time was causing havoc to my sense of reality. I stood still for a second and drew in a deep breath to avoid retching. Vertigo overcame me, but I held back the fear and faced the Elementarae.

He looked concerned as he made the machinations for another attack. I think he was wondering why I had not responded with my own spell. Still, he seemed determined to end the duel as quickly as he could by way of a powerful casting.

I felt this one build up as well. I tried to focus on the finer details of the spell, which I was learning to discern. New flavors of clove and pepper added to the fish and cabbage stew which he was brewing. An undertone of turnip, or maybe radish, left me feeling slightly famished.

I think I was trying to drink in the flavors, to sample each nuance of the casting in order to understand the man who I was facing. To be honest I was not really thinking my way through at this point I was simply letting the experience happen. My reactions were nothing more than uncontrolled responses to his actions.

The blast of energy shot out toward me. The force of it was so great that I mentally stumbled. Physically I stumbled too. The pulse hit me then stopped entirely. The world no longer moved outside the envelope of the spell which was seeking to destroy me.

Again, I saw the fabric of the spell made up of waves of light and ripples of air. A conical spear of ice floated in the center. I stepped aside to let it pass. Had I not done so it would have impaled me through the heart. The world went fast speed again. And again, back to a relatively easy pace. The ice spike crashed against a concrete column some twenty yards behind me.

I was beginning to feel less nausea at the shifting of my perception, but the added scents and flavors of the magic began to overwhelm me. A deeper burnt spice became apparent as my opponent readied his next casting.

He was obviously going out of his element now as the flame spread slowly from his hands. It crawled up his arms a short way then began to well up like water overflowing a cup. The blaze rushed towards me before it contacted the ground.

By instinct, I reached out my hands to ward off the heat. I was surprised that there was not actually any heat to be felt. I could see the air ripple as though a great furnace were active. The flames washed around my hands leaving me unmolested.

I had not expected to be immune from this attack. I could feel the power, and indeed I knew that the flames were searing the very air around me. Still, I stood unaffected. I realized in that moment that I somehow had turned the power that had charged the spell from its shape to an unshaped thing. A feeling of elation and understanding overcame me all at one.

I stepped toward the Elementarae. He hesitated for a moment. I could see the doubt in his face. A palpable fear rose from him, and the taste of his magic was suddenly sweet and cloying.

Without waiting for another spell to be cast, I rushed toward him in a sprint. He feverishly worked another spell, but I knew he could not complete the semantics before I reached him. As I stepped into range, I balled up my fist and punched him hard in the jaw.

He slumped to the floor in a heap. A deep sigh escaped him as he lost consciousness. I looked down upon him for a moment then stepped back and turned toward Janis.

Time sped up suddenly and I lost my sense of the world. I felt myself retch as darkness took me. The last thing I remember was the twisting pain in my wrist as it desperately tried to stop my fall.

I awoke covered in sweat and vomit. The stench elicited another gag, but I held back and swallowed the bile. Pain shot through my arm and the back of my head. I felt a warm wet sensation indicating that I'd cracked my skull against the floor when I'd fallen.

Janis knelt next to me. I heard her speak soft words, and I tasted the honey and cinnamon of the spell she was using to heal me. The pain quickly subsided from my head and wrist. A throbbing pulse remained to remind me of my brush with death.

"You will be alright," her matronly tone surprised me.

"What happened?" were the only words that came to my slightly aching head.

"You did as I expected. You were able to dissemble his spells."

"What does that mean?"

"Only a few of the highest placed guild members know about this. Under other circumstances, I would never tell you this fact," she paused to think for a moment. "Some like you, who can sense magic, also have the ability to diffuse the effects of any given spell by what we call dissembling. Or, in other words, you separate the various components of a spell, the power, from the focus, from the effect. I had a suspicion about you from the first time we met. It was one of the reasons I wanted you as my partner. Having the ability to feel is useful, add the ability to render a spell useless..."

"You knew I could do this?" I asked incredulous.

"No. I suspected. I hoped. I've only heard of this effect before, and only in one person. There are legends of people from the dark times who could do this, but they are unsubstantiated. I hoped that the intense magical conflict might expose this ability and I was correct. I believe you must be highly focused for it to work," she paused for a moment as if considering her next words carefully.

"Do you remember what you experienced during the duel?"

I thought for a moment before replying. “I think that I perceived time flowing differently, fast then slow, then fast again, as though...” I tried to find the right words. “It was as though I could sense the spell reaching for me and slow it down. Maybe during the slow parts I was somehow able to ward off the spell.”

“Ward is not the correct term, but I guess it will serve,” she smiled. “I watched using my seeing spell. What you actually did, was to segregate the spell. Each part of the casting was disentangled from the spell. Any machine is built of thousands of parts working together. For magic it is the same. Once separated there is no spell, only power and focus and intent with nothing to bind them.”

“I remember seeing or maybe tasting separate parts, and, I saw or sensed a sort of rainbow as time slowed for me. I tasted individual flavors. You know how I do? It felt as though each color, each taste, each feeling was easy to separate. Like understanding the ingredients of a pot of soup. I guess? I think I understand now.”

"Either way you are free of the geas. You have fought the duel and won. Our friend here is also free. I sense no other residual traces of the summoning on him. Perhaps we should find out who he is," she helped me up.

We looked down at the man, studying him for a moment. Janis knelt and riffled through his pockets. She retrieved a wallet and a small set of keys with about a half dozen on a ring.

On his right-hand middle finger was a large ring of gold and silver with the crest of some family prominently displayed in black lacquer. The shape of a leopard guardant facing the sinister reminded me of European nobility. A red border surrounded the shield shape. I had the idea I had seen it before. He also carried a number of small personal items. These included a comb and pocket mirror.

I decided not to cuff him, as he lay there unconscious. We'd have time enough to determine whether to charge him and with what. I could sense a lightly placed, honey flavored spell, flowing around him. Janis must have given him a sleep cast. If so, he would be out for hours, unless she let it abate.

Janis opened the large leather wallet which was embossed with the same leopard crest as the ring. The driving license and magical practitioner certificate gave us the name of Jordan Marnovitev. He was a highly placed water wizard of the Elementarae guild. According to the certificate, he held the post of high adjudicator of the guild.

An adjudicator was generally responsible for discipline and order within the guild. Should a member break the code or bylaws of the guild, his punishment would be in the hands of this man. The system was pretty convoluted though. There would be many levels of bureaucracy which meant he himself was probably rarely involved in the majority of cases. Only the most important disciplinary actions would warrant his involvement.

I seemed to remember a recent kerfuffle within the guild, which had something to do with its newer members wishing to explore more modern elemental skills, based on a combination of old philosophical elemental practice and more modern physical science.

The results were a split within the guild that was only solved by the creation of a smaller separate union of metaphysical scientists. In short, they had been kicked out of the guild. I remember reading that this man was responsible for the expulsion of the dissenters.

I also remember seeing him in the papers, and on screen rambling on about the purity of the cause of the guild and its work.

He impressed me with his style of speaking, which tended to rile people up, either for or against his arguments. His personality was divisive, and his rhetoric elicited the worst responses from people.

I was glad I had been able to beat him in the duel. I felt a sense of satisfaction, perhaps a little vindictive. A lowly dud had topped this high honored caster. I could not hide my smug smile.

Janis noticed and smiled in return. She knew what I was thinking, and I knew her attitude towards people like him as well. One of the few times we saw eye to eye was on elitism within Caster society.

Janis held that casters were no better or worse than non-casters. They were who they were not based on their ability but based on their choices. She had once told me that she thought it was our decisions that made us powerful or weak. It was our choices which made us either good or evil.

I tended to agree, but like most non-casters, I held a certain awe for those with the ability. To Janis non-casters were like people who could not see the color green. In general, it really didn't matter. Casters might see green, but they often didn't see past their own ego.

In either case, the man lying there was one of those that looked down his nose, not only at non-casters, but at those he deemed to be beneath him within the cast system of his own guild, a genuine elitist. It was for that reason I felt the smugness.

We had no evidence that he'd killed anyone, and the taste of his magic was different than the residual left at the murder scene in the underground. At best, we could charge him with illegal dueling, but, in the same terms, I could also be charged with that, even under a magical geas. His defense might be that he was under the same compulsion.

Without the ability to link him to the actual creation of the spell which created the geas, we would have a hard time convicting him of anything. It might be possible to detangle the various elements of the ritual and see his magical footprint in the spells design. I offered this as an opinion to Janis.

She felt that the spell would take too long to deconstruct, and by then she might be dead from the effect of the spell. Instead, she felt we should follow the leads and see who else was involved. In that way, we might be able to build a conspiracy case as well as the illegal dueling charge. We would also discover the murderer. More importantly, our course of action was to remove the deadly geas from her. We had less than three hours to see to it.

So far, we had found a member from Children of Hermes and the Elementarae. Members from the five other guilds would be involved. Checking the backgrounds of those we knew, and comparing them against each other, might provide clues to the unknown five.

I suggested that to Janis. We agreed to head back to the station and spend no more than an hour doing research. After that, she was sure, that her geas would begin to draw her to the next member of the illegal dueling ring.

Less than ten minutes found us at our terminals. I spent some time compiling information of each person and set the display to show the murdered victim on the left and our captured duelist on the right of the screen.

Janis took our suspect down to intake and booked him in on charges of dueling and conspiracy. Even if we could not prove the charges, he'd be out of circulation for the better part of the day which would remove him from dueling long enough for the thing to be over. I had thought to go with attempted murder as well, but she talked me out of it. I knew she'd be gone most of the hour doing the necessary paperwork.

Under other conditions, she'd have left the administrative duties with me. I was generally better at the research side of our work. She wanted to maximize our chances of getting information.

I could not blame her. It was her life on the line now. I felt a strange sense of responsibility to her now. Knowing that she was in danger emphasized the fact that even with all her powers as a caster she was still human and vulnerable. Maybe I was seeing her in a different light now due to my recent discovery of the true nature of my own abilities.

I felt a profound sense of self-confidence. I know that in many ways it was unwarranted. Being essentially immune to the effects of a spell was liberating. Still, it was something I had to concentrate on to make it work. I could probably be caught unawares. Maybe the elated feeling was a false security. For now, I wanted to feel the invincibility.

Jordan Marnovitev and Johnathon Albertage had very little in common.

The doctor was late middle aged with a somewhat liberal mindset. He'd been involved in organizations linked to his profession and his particular passion pertaining to equality and aiding the poor and homeless. In most every aspect he was someone that I could not ever imagine being involved in a secret dueling society.

His wife was a caster as well. She belonged to the Talismantecha, but was a low-level factory caster who spent most of her time on the assembly line as a quality control manager. I imagined that she did this because she enjoyed the work. Albertage would easily have made enough money to fulfill whatever needs and wants they might have.

Marnovitev was a somewhat less sympathetic character. He obviously considered himself to be superior to most people around him. He'd advocated for stricter laws regulating the use of magic, and a separation of social identity between the magical and non-magical professions.

To be sure, there was already something of a segregation by virtue of the inherent requirements of industry. I wondered how he would interpret me within his socio-political theology.

My mental rambling was cut short when I realized there was a very strong connection between them in that they had both been involved in the youth of the casting community. Particularly, they represented their own guilds in 'The Choosing'.

When a child is discovered to have any magical abilities, they would be put through a series of tests which were meant to determine the best guild for them to join. Afterward, they'd be apprenticed and educated by that guild until they became adepts within the guild. There were often occasions wherein a child might have potential matches with more than one guild. In these cases, a representative of the potential guild would entice the child and their parents. Often the guild resorted to payments to the parents to choose one guild over the other. Depending on the talent of the child, these bidding wars sometimes made a family wealthy.

The guild reps who did this kind of recruiting were known as the 'Gatherers'. Each of these men were one of the local 'Gatherers' for their respective guild.

As a matter of course, I recorded the names of the Gatherers for all the guilds. It turned out that there were about half dozen for each guild. After eliminating the known two, I began to compare the remaining guild representatives against Albertage and Marnovitev.

One thing that surprised me, though I suppose that it shouldn't have, is that Janis was one of the Chavezen Gatherers. I obliged by keeping her name on the list. Perhaps she would have some insight into that particular clue.

While no other single thing connected the two, I made several one or two step connections which looked promising. Both men had high incomes. I divided the other gatherers into lists based on wealth and on the organizations they belonged too. I even made a listing of the churches or religious organizations, and two-level family trees, to see if there might be any relationship that would provide a clue.

I even sorted the potential candidates by birthday and age. I reasoned that there could well be an astrological connection. Both the known duelists were born in August. Of the other gatherers, only two had similar birth months. Ages ranged from 33 to 89. Janis was the youngest.

I drew out a chart with each of the potential duelists along one edge and began to tree them together based on all the factors I'd come up with so far. There wasn't anything I could find that connected more than four of them except their roles as Gatherers. I was even more convinced that we would end up having to wait for the next murder, or for Janis to face someone before I could make any connections.

By now Janis had returned. I showed her my progress and hoped she might have insight into the case.

"Gatherers," she smiled. "I knew I recognized Albertage," her smile widened. "I've never directly interacted with Marnovitev, but by your information, he is the head of Gatherers for his guild so he would only have been directly involved for a 'potential' with high connections or of strong ability. It is kind of an elitist group, these Gatherers. They like to think of themselves as recruiting the future."

"And you?" I asked. "Do you know any of the others and how they might be connected?"

“Knowing this information, I would guess that they all went after a particularly versatile ‘potential’. Maybe there is some kind of unknown competition between them that can only be resolved by way of duels to the death,” she mused. “It wouldn’t be sanctioned by the Guilds, but it might be related to recruitment.”

“Is there an official organization or association to the gatherers?” I wondered. “I mean, how does one know who they are meant to recruit?”

“Generally, all gatherers are assigned by the head Gatherer of each guild. That is how it works in the Chavezen guild. I assume it is similar in the others. I’m usually assigned to the very young children who are discovered. I think it is because I’m one of the younger Gatherers. For the more complex cases, my mentor William Airensten would be the one. A couple of the others for our guild take the less high profile ‘potentials’. And we have one person who handles the special cases.”

“Special cases?” I asked.

“It happens sometimes that a ‘potential’ is discovered who has a developmental disability such as a physical handicap, or emotional challenge or mental disability, that sort of thing. These require very special handling, and the Gatherers who manage these cases are specially trained. These special gatherers also are brought in when a child is identified who has immense potential, well beyond the typical caster.”

“How do we find out if any of those on the list have that training? We could at least eliminate that as a common thread.”

“I could make a few calls,” she smiled. “I think you might be on to something.” She sat at her desk across from me and began making calls.

I went back to my list and added a line item for the head gatherers. That didn’t offer anything, since Albertage was not the head gatherer for his guild. On a whim, I accessed articles on guild recruitment and discovered something which seemed important. Both of our current duelists had been involved at a national conference on youth in the guilds about seven months ago. A sub-committee of gatherers from the area had been sent to represent the local concerns. I made a list of everyone who had attended. Each guild had sent at least two representatives. I remembered that Janis had gone as the junior member of her guild. The list was now potentially whittled to just over twenty if this was a clue.

Janis had some luck on her first few calls and informed me she had a real lead. I was elated to find that all the special need's gatherers were on my list of attendees. Although the link was tenuous, we had something to go on. I had a hunch we were on to something. As I've said before, my hunches were usually spot on.

Our list might be reduced to these seven persons. The two we already knew of being Albertage and Marnovitev.

The Chavezen guild's special gatherer was Dr. Fromale. He was an older man in his early sixties. There was nothing particularly notable about him other than having been assigned as a gatherer for most of his career.

The Talismantecha guild had a new specialist since the recent head of the local guild had been incarcerated recently. Donna Brackenshith was young and apparently highly ambitious. At 37, she was the youngest on the now narrowed list of potential suspects.

Crendal Vemendall seemed to be something of a mystery. Most members of the Necromages guild cultivated this impression, and he seemed to have taken it to the next level. His face was hidden deep in hoods in the one picture I was able to find of him. Only a thin-lipped mouth and the black and white eyes were clearly visible.

I could not find anything other than the name of the Naturalist, Tony McMannon. Listing him was purely functional. Apparently, naturalists do not like to have their pictures taken.

A full military dressed Helda Platt represented the military guild. Though there were several photos of her, everyone presented her with an impassive expression. She seemed unperturbed by any situation. I could imagine the calm demeanor in the face of the worst crisis.

Just as I wrote down her name as a primary, a call came over my phone from the dispatch desk. There had been another murder.

Death by magic is usually a nasty business. In this case, it was downright messy as well.

The room was perhaps a hundred feet long and half that wide. Mezzanine's stood two levels high on either side of the long central area where tables formed three parallel lines the length of the room. Everywhere I looked I could see books and scrolls. This was the main library of Seattle's Mystical Arts University.

The roof and upper walls were stained glass designs representing the evolution of magical education over the last four thousand years. Each ten-foot panel was dedicated to a major event. I was surprised to see two of them graphically depicting the Caster Wars.

It was due to these two events, the most recent only a century ago, that modern society was possible. Had the last war not ended in stalemate, either caster or normal people would have been subjugated or even obliterated. In truth, it was sheer numbers that allowed the non-casters to maintain their equality. Only perhaps one tenth of one percent of everyone born has any casting ability, and of those less that ten percent are capable of more than simple spells.

As I reflected on this, I found I was somewhat glad that the balance was such as it was. I didn't like the idea of either group finding itself in a position where they could dictate to the other. I'd seen enough power hungry and power drunk people in my life. In my line of work, I met the worst of both worlds. People broke the law for any of the three basic reasons: Passion, power, or wealth.

When I looked for a motive for a crime, I could always find it in one of the three. Passion covers a lot of ground. Hate, love, fear, even momentary madness, were all passionate "reasons" for crime. Power and wealth, they are self-explanatory.

The central section of the library seemed to have been used as a dueling ground. About a third of the way in from the western entrance, floating in midair above the center row of tables, was a mass of red and black.

As we entered the room, I sensed a change in Janis. Her demeanor seemed to relax from the normal slightly uptight, to a sort of resigned sadness. She was usually pretty closed off with her emotions. I supposed the job could get to anyone after a while. Maybe it was the graphic nature of the murder.

Blood splatters covered much of the area. The victim had been cut thousands of times. Each injury created its own random pattern of red dots across whatever surfaces and objects were within the radius of effect. Though the injuries were not deep or long, the total effect was grizzly. Not an inch of the body was not covered with cuts, making identification difficult.

As I looked around, I was somewhat surprised by the almost exact circle of blood. The floor, the bookshelves, the tables, each showed the strange geometry which indicated a specific radius of the spells effect.

The residual magical aura tasted of iron and rye. There was an almost artificial flavor to it which caused me to wonder about the caster. It is true I was wondering about the caster anyway. But in this case, I felt as though they'd used some sort of focus for the spell. Something not natural.

Janis was doing her detection spells as usual, so I wandered the scene looking for anything that might be important.

The death had obviously occurred here. It seemed odd that a place as public as this would have been the site of a magical duel, and I made a mental note to discuss that subject with Janis when she was finished with her routine.

It was nearing noon and I also wondered when this had happened, and why the library had not been full of students at the time of the duel. Even at off hours, university libraries might have students catching up on studies or cramming for tests.

I found the librarian who'd called in the crime. She was a younger grad student. Her slight frame and nearly white hair made her seem, at first glance, to be much older. Smooth skin and a sort of naive bearing told me the truth.

She introduced herself as Carmen Montel. She didn't seem too distraught by finding the dead body, or the state of it. I discovered she was a member of the Chavezen guild who had been gathered by Janis some years ago. Obviously, her clear head and calm demeanor served her well as a member of that particular group.

“Was there anyone else in the library during the morning?” I asked.

“The library was closed today for a convocation. It happens on occasion. Several scholars will want to research some specific topic and request the library for a private session. Dr. Fromale was the requesting party,” she motioned toward the still floating corpse.

“Did he indicate who else was part of the convocation?”

“I’ll have to look over the records. They aren’t required to record the members of the convocation. Only one member of the faculty needs to sign off, and that was Dr. Fromale.”

“Which guild was he associated with?”

“He was a Chavezen, like me. This university specialized in three areas of study. Law and

Chavezen magic, elemental magic, and magical history. The first two are sponsored by the respective guilds, and magical history is a general studies department which is supported by the entire caster community."

As I was interviewing Carmen, three black suited people entered the library from the opposite double doors. I noticed them out of the corner of my eye, but I immediately knew them to be guild police.

I recognized the tall man with black hair and eyes and a slight build named Thomas Drakkin. He was a Chavezen. Janis and he had a genial working relationship. He'd helped on a couple of cases in the past.

A heavy-set woman in her late thirties wore a polyester pant suit which was pale blue with red threaded pockets. I could make out the large lapel pin indicating her association with the Elementarae.

I did not recognize the other man who was much older and wore a dark gray pinstripe. I got a sour taste in my mouth from him. He exuded tamarind and horseradish. I later discovered he was also from the Elementarae guild.

They waited patiently for Janis to complete her initial casting then
Thomas introduced the other Guild police. Janis motioned for me to join them. I asked Carmen to wait there and walked over to the gathered casters.

“Jack,” Thomas nodded to me in solicitude.

The others ignored me.

“Thomas. It’s good to see you again. How have you been?” I replied.

He nodded and continued his conversation with Janis.

“So, as I was saying, we’ve been directed to interface with you on the case. Since this happened on Guild territory, which is shared by the hosts of the University, each guild will have representation. This is Michael Norvorst and Nancy Dremont of the Elementarae. Also, in light of the report you filed earlier about the murder in the underground, it was decided that you would lead the investigation, even though we would normally have jurisdiction of the actual crime here."

He looked like he was holding back a smile. I got the sense that he'd convinced the other guild police, perhaps against their will, that it should be handled this way. There was some unspoken signal between him and Janis which made me wonder if she was already aware of the conditions.

I offered my hand to each of them in turn and went over what we had discovered in a pretty succinct way. I left out the geas which Janis was still under and the details of my recent "duel".

We then began to walk the room looking for anything which might excite our attention. Overall, the library was somewhat sterile. Other than the body and the blood, we found nothing to indicate who else might be involved.

A quick check with Janis informed us that Dr. Fromale was the special needs gatherer for the Chavezens. This was the clue that started to bring the picture together. Now we could narrow the focus on only those gatherers. Hopefully we would find a connection.

In that moment I began to wonder if this whole thing was a sort of competition for control of a specific child. Could it be that they were fighting to gather a particularly powerful or interesting special needs prospect.

We invited the guild investigators to come to our office and review the reports and clues we'd gathered so far.

As we exited the library, I voiced my opinion about the special needs gatherers to Janis. Her silent nod told me I was probably closer to the mark than I could have known. It also showed me that there was some bit of information she had which I did not. I didn't like the idea of being left out.

Our stroll to her car was quiet. The guild investigators climbed into the roomy back seat while I took shotgun. Janis would never let me drive her fancy flit.

"Do you think this is all because of some kid that everyone wanted in their guild?" I asked Janis.

"It is a distinct possibility," she nodded. "In the old tradition, duels would sometimes resolve these disputes. It is also true that laws against dueling have been in place since the great war."

"So, if that is it, these people are not really all that concerned about the legality of the act?" I asked.

"Or the reward outweighs the potential punishment," she replied. "Casters often feel themselves above the law anyway. It is an undesirable side effect of having so much power. And the more powerful, the less likely the law seems to interest a person."

"I'm surprised you said that," I smiled.

"Just because I'm a caster does not mean I feel that way as well. Chavezens are mostly respectful of the law even if there is a feeling of being above it. Laws are meant to keep society from collapsing. And to maintain a safety net for less powerful. I mean that in the way of non-casters and casters alike. Non-casters who have power can be just as dismissive of the law as a caster. It just seems more pressing when it is a caster because of the ramifications. The truth is, anyone with power over another should wield it with respect and humility."

I was reminded by her attitude the main reason I respected her. There were times where I felt awe because of her abilities. There were times when I thought her methods were either too rigorous or too heavy handed. But she was always thoughtful about why she did what she did. I wondered if I could live up to that standards and realized I had often fallen short.

Maybe she was so much more rigorous than most because of the responsibility she felt over using her powers. Since I couldn't do what she could, I could be less strict in my methods. Was it really a distinction though?

As a police officer, I had power which might be just as impactful as a single spell. Guilt welled in me as I ran through these thoughts. I resolved to be more mindful.

As far as Janis went, her time was running out. I knew she would be feeling the pull of the geas much harder now. It was only a matter of time before she would be forced to engage in a duel which could potentially be deadly.

When we returned to the office, Janis and I set up a conference room to go over what we had so far with the new team members. I decided to look at them that way and hoped we could have a smooth relationship. I was also aware that most of the guild police looked at people like me as a sort of freak at best, and a subhuman animal at worst.

These guys seemed to be holding their tongues, if that was the case, and it suited me since I really wasn't in the mood for anything which would distract from the investigation at hand.

After a brief rundown on our findings, the discussion evolved into a commentary on the aspects of gathering, and why that might be a focal point in the investigation. As Janis was the only one of the four of us with any understanding of the vocation, we let her lead the discussion. She went straight to the point by talking about why a special needs gatherer might get involved in a potential.

"Really, many reasons might call for a special needs gatherer. The first is any kind of condition which might make it difficult to integrate the potential into normal guild training programs. That might include any form or autism or ADHD. As it turns out, lots of magically gifted people are highly obsessive and compulsive, or might have social disconnection issues including megalomania or schizoid tendencies. Down syndrome and other learning disabilities might call for special needs. In general, there is a threshold of whether or not the candidate can be integrated easily into an apprenticeship. Maybe one in twenty require special handling, and maybe one in a hundred require a special needs gatherer to mentor them through the initiation process. These are then given over to a mentor who will train them one on one till they are passed as adepts. At least that is the way it works in the Chavezen guild. I imagine there are similar methods in each of the other guilds."

Her description of the process made it seem a little archaic to me, but so much of the magical community was highly traditional and old fashioned. I had several thoughts about the next step, but I kept them to myself so that I didn't interfere with the conversation.

Janis Continued.

"Another reason you might expect a special needs gatherer would be if the family of the prospect was high status. Wealthy or political families almost always end up in the special needs category. This is because they require some amount of tact and finesse to bring in the candidate."

"The only other time a special needs gatherer is brought in is in the case of illness. Either magical or mundane maladies which could infect or affect others. Or diseases which require special handling such as quarantine or isolation from others. Or special devices to support the initiate," Janis stopped for a moment. A look of concern flashed quickly across her face before she continued. "These things might vary somewhat between the guilds but in general..." She trailed off.

Janis was running out of time. There were only around two hours before she'd be required to duel. I knew the pull on her would be terrible by now as I had only felt it briefly, I could imagine the force of will it must take for her not to obey the geas.

“How do we go about contacting the other gatherers and determining if they might be involved. I mean, if we want to confirm the theory?” I interjected.

“I suggest Jack and Thomas talk to the Via De Natural gatherer then the Necromage. Michael, Nancy and I will talk to the Talismantecha, and after that we all go to the Aresinia guilder,” Janis suggested.

“You want to face the most dangerous with all of us to back you up, is that it?” Norvorst snarled.

I couldn’t tell if he was trying to bait Janis or not. If so, she did not take his remark that way.

“He is the most dangerous. If we manage to capture the others before the time limit expires, we might need all of our abilities to bring him in,” she paused and sighed slowly. “If what we suspect is true.”

Several assumptions were made about the locations of each gatherer. A few phone calls later and we knew where to find the naturalist, Talismantecha, and the Aresinia guilds members but the Necromage was not in the office or at home.

I was worried over Janis. She seemed to be pushing it to the edge as far as time went. If we didn't get each of the gatherers quickly, she might end up in mortal peril. I was relieved when she pulled me aside and told me she'd managed to contact her friend who could possibly stem the fatal effects from the geas.

As we split up, Thomas and I headed to the Naturalists compound which amounted to nothing so much as a forested encampment in the middle of the city. It took us only a few minutes to drive over the hill in the checked out unmarked flit. The area south of Seward Park had been cordoned off with a large hedge of hawthorn and juniper. The immaculately trimmed wall of green stood more than ten feet tall and was interrupted along Westlake drive by a walking gate with several parking stalls along the street. No vehicles were allowed in the enclave.

The adept at the gate allowed our entry and informed us that Prefect McMannon was receiving visitors in the herb garden. Thomas shuddered with a slight chill as we crossed the threshold.

A mix of blueberries and pine needles came into my mind. A barrier spell might be guarding the entrance. It tasted like a defensive barrier anyway. I'm not sure how I knew.

The Herb Garden was a short walk from the gate. The tall thin man was standing near the center of the open area ringed by dozens of planters, each containing a range of plants. From where I stood, I could tell the planters were arranged in groups of three. Each bore either the symbol for water, air, or earth. I learned later that these three resources were considered the power behind all natural magic.

Immediately, I could tell that McMannon was prepared for a confrontation. His hands were just away from his hips in a sort of ready position. I sensed his focus and could taste the sweetness and earthiness of his magic already beginning to build.

"McMannon. We are not here to challenge you," Thomas said loudly. We were still more than twenty yards away and he wanted to make sure he was heard.

"We are investigating the deaths of two casters and a possible dueling ring. Do you want to talk to us, or shall we bring you into the station?"

McMannon seemed unmoved. He flexed his fingers and Thomas yelped in surprise as tendrils of roots wrapped around his ankles, holding him fast.

"My business is with that one," McMannon said as he pointed to me.

I realized, perhaps too late, that I, though I had been freed of the geas of the duel, still might have been marked by it. Maybe it wasn't about one fight but about being the last duelist standing.

The spell was not as powerful as I expected. It was subtle though. It took me a few seconds to realize he was already casting.

I could feel the flow of the spell as it cascaded across the garden and knew he had chosen this spot as his for a dueling ground for a reason.

The power flowed through the plants and through the ground toward me. The lines between the components were almost undetectable. But there in a small clear taste of salty water. I felt the connection and unbound it. McMannon's spell died out without ever having shown its effect.

I stepped toward him and said in a loud voice, "We don't have to do this. I've already had one duel and I'd like to avoid another if I can. Just talk to us."

The next spell was all power and no substance. I separated the components easily. They tasted of sage and rosemary. I knew the spell would have ripped open my gut had it managed to reach me. I think he was working on small plant matter in my stomach, trying to make it grow.

A realization dawned on me. I could sense a coldness and a deep desire from this one. It felt as though he needed to use his magic. Like a drug, he had become so addicted to the feeling of power, the enhanced connection to the flow of magic, that he could not resist using it even if he'd wanted too. In that instance I felt sorry for him.

I knew it was something that Janis and I would discuss later. I wondered if it was something that happened often in the caster community. If this thing worked out where neither of us ended up dead, I'd want to see if there was some support system for people like him.

I took another step toward him as he staggered backward now fearing for his life. "Don't come closer," he yelled.

"I'm not going to let this go on," I replied in a calm voice. "Yield and it will end."

"I cannot yield. The child should be here. It is the only place where he can know peace," he replied.

His plea confirmed my suspicion. The revelation that the dueling geas was over a prospect was what Janis and I suspected all along. If only I could stop him before I had to hurt him. Or before he managed to get a spell to affect me.

"I don't care where he goes," I needed to know who he was talking about. "Dueling is no way of determining his fate." Again, I closed the distance.

"The others will use him, to hurt, to cause trouble. He doesn't understand what it means. He will never understand," McMannon's voice was cracking. I could sense the genuine pain he felt thinking about the boy's fate. "Here he can have peace and never know pain of the discipline."

I was only a few yards away now and McMannon had not seemed inclined to cast another spell. I continued to talk in soothing tones hoping to keep him from blasting me to oblivion.

"His fate should be determined by those that love him best. He should be free to make the choice for himself," Now only a few feet from McMannon.

McMannon lowered his head in defeat.

"He doesn't understand. How can he? Even his own family would use him for their own ends. His own father..." he sighed. "I yield."

I could feel the weight of the geas drop from him. His shoulders relaxed and his face dropped into an expression of worry. McMannon touched a fern nearby and smiled sadly as it grew several inches.

“You have to help him,” he said in a voice so low I almost couldn’t hear. “He just needs peace.” He touched a yellow and black flower and smiled again as it bloomed.

Office of the Colonel

Janis and her team found themselves sitting in a waiting room which was both posh and sterile. Costly white and gray carpets matched the wood and leather furniture. The walls were decorated with paintings of famous military casters and certificates of rank or achievement. The heavy double door which led to the inner office was guarded by a stern looking middle aged woman in the uniform of an officer of the Aresinia. She sported several rows of ribbons and the rank of major on her overly ornate uniform.

The benches upon which Janis and her companions sat was of hard wicker and wood. They threatened to brake whenever one of them adjusted their sitting position in an attempt to get more comfortable. The squeak was a loud reminder that neither security nor comfort were to be found in the office of the commander of the recruitment battalion.

The ten-minute wait was rewarded with a beeping from a communication panel on the major's desk, which signaled the receptionist that her superior was ready to receive visitors. Janis stood quickly. She seemed in a hurry. Her time was running out.

The Colonel stood to receive the three in silence, then motioned to several chairs arraigned across from her desk.

Janis quickly moved forward to interpose herself and spoke in a forced clarity to ensure that there would be no confusion about the meaning of her words.

"Before we start ma'am, I would warn you, as you know, I am bound by the same compulsion as you. I, however, came to be involved by accident, and would ask the favor of Simplex Provocare."

The officer smiled and nodded unbuttoning the top button on her tunic, "You first," she said in a deep voice laced with confidence.

Janis cast a cutting spell which opened a small injury on the neck the officer had just exposed. The colonel smiled and returned the casting creating an exact copy of the slash on Janis's neck.

"I yield," Janis said quietly bowing her head.

The duel was over.

"You took a big chance," The voice echoed. "By right of the duel I could have easily killed you?"

"You are honorable," Janis pulled a handkerchief from her breast pocket and dabbed at the blood. "It was a gamble, I suppose. I have no interest in your duel except that several people have already been injured or killed for it."

"Oh yes, that is true, but the reasons are far more intriguing than you might have imagined. And though dueling in general is illegal, we were forced to the point by the stubbornness of the father who set the terms of the gathering. The child is too important to let his fate be decided any other way," she sat down facing her visitors.

She motioned for them to sit.

Janis took the chair to the right, indicating her position as leader of the group. The others seemed inclined to keep their positions subservient to hers, for this meeting at least.

"I need to know the name of the child and family and want to validate the other members of the duel," Janis went straight to the point.

This was a tactic that Colonel Platt seemed to like. She pulled a tissue from an ornate box near the left of her desk and folded it several times before placing it over the cut and buttoning up over it. The time she spent seemed to be innocuous, but Janis felt she was using the few seconds to think about how she should answer.

After Platt sat, she looked across at each of her visitors, in turn, starting from the left and ending with Janis.

“Unfortunately, I am not able to reveal any details of the challenge due to the magic used. We made sure that none of us would be able to betray the others. However, you seemed to have already surmised much, and I am happy to oblige with either confirmation or denial of any assumed facts.”

Janis was not surprised by the security included in the dueling spell. She had hoped that since she was inadvertently pulled into the duel, she might be free of this compulsion. If so, the Colonel was not willing to come clean in any way, which might betray her own sense of honor.

Janis decided the direct tact had worked so far and set to the questions as though she were interviewing a job applicant.

“All the participants in the duel are special needs Gatherers?” she prodded.

“Yes” no hint of emotion was present in the answer.

“This whole thing is because of a prospect?”

“Yes,” again, her reply was flat.

“Are this child’s parents aware of the duel?”

"That one I cannot answer, as it is obvious you do not yet know the full details. As I said, I can either confirm or deny assumed facts. You are asking a direct question."

Janis thought for a moment, then continued the interrogation.

"As a special needs prospect, the child is both incapable of understanding the situation and very powerful?" she decided to take a different tac.

"As to the first, I will not say, because you have no idea. The second is obvious. If the prospect were not powerful, we wouldn't feel the need to fight over this one," The Colonel smiled as she stared into Janis's eyes.

"None of this was your idea?" Janis realized.

"Correct," she replied. "However, once the decision was taken, I agreed to enter for the good of the prospect and the Aresinia."

"Outside of the fact that this is illegal, how did you think this was going to end? I mean you can't have thought this to have been a good idea," Janis prodded.

“I was prepared to risk a great deal for my order and for the child. In the end I will not be prosecuted no matter the outcome. But I will probably lose my status as commander of the local guild and as gather. I reasoned the reward was great enough to risk it,”

“No matter the outcome, you knew you could lose your honor and your status and did it anyway?” Janis was shocked. “One prospect cannot be that valuable.”

“Oh, but if you knew,” she nodded. “You would do anything to bring this particular prospect into your guild. If for no other reason than keeping the power from the other guilds. That is how powerful this child could be.”

“You would train them to be a weapon. What kind of life is that for a child?” Janis accused the officer.

“I doubt that would have been the case. My recommendation would be to only train the prospect in defensive casting, healing, that sort of thing,”

“Even if their potential was so much greater?”

"Even so."

"Why?"

"I won't answer that either, as it is information you do not have," Another emotionless smile. "Confirm or deny, but not fill in the blanks. That is my deal."

"Okay," Janis was clearly beginning to get flustered.

There was so much information she wanted to get. She knew The Colonel had the answers. It was just a matter of asking the right questions.

"I'll infer that the child is either mentally or emotionally challenged because you would essentially neutralize whatever power the child has knowing it will be difficult to control," Janis said almost under her breath.

"Correct," Colonel Platt replied, "Or socially challenged. I'll elaborate, because I'm feeling you should understand this one point. This child would not be a good candidate for advanced training which could be used to harm others. That is my dilemma. I wish to maintain safety above all. The child not the least. Should a person with this much potential power be left to their own devices or allowed to follow normal training from any of the guilds, it could mean danger."

Janis was beginning to get a picture of a troubled child who might be easily manipulated, or perhaps had trouble with temper control. In any case, Platt was probably right. This prospect should not be treated as a normal initiate. The consequences could be grave.

She began to wonder about the parents. Under other conditions they would have the biggest input into where the child would be placed. With a special needs initiate, thought was given to the requirements, and sometimes a parent's desires might be overridden. Janis had never seen that happen before, but there was precedent. It occurred to her that the guild duel was taking on itself to override any other avenue of choice that might otherwise be available to the child.

She supposed that this might be best but felt a certain distain for the process, due to its inherently forceful nature. In her mind, choice was the most valuable of the freedoms a person might have. The right of choice in vocation felt almost sacred.

“Does this child have a choice in the matter? Are you all just ignoring what the family thinks?” Janis asked. Her tone was sharper than she’d meant it to be.

“The father has made no preference shown. He is a very low-level caster in Talismantecha, which would otherwise have recommended the child there. However, his limited abilities and the fact that the child’s mother passed away early in his life has meant that there should be an intervention, and the decision has been taken by our duel. According to ancient rule, the challenge was invoked,” The Colonel insisted.

“The challenge was not meant to be a duel to the death. It was meant to be a test of skills,” Janis replied. “Further, the rule of challenge was dismissed by the guild court more than 150 years ago, after the first guild war ended. Rules of gathering were developed to prevent exactly such an occasion as this.”

“Before we even decided upon the duel, we all knew that any other method would not suffice. Each of us felt too strongly about our position on the candidate. Should this child be placed wrongly, we might all suffer. Those that took upon themselves the challenge, are willing to risk life and position to bring the child into our guild. I know, each has our own desire for the child's future. Some will try to use the child in the hope that good will come from the power, others will try to minimize the child's influence and education to limit the potential harm. There has even been discussion of deconditioning the child," Platt replied.

Deconditioning meant magically lobotomizing the aspirant. Essentially cutting the child off from magic altogether in order to prevent possible tragedy. This was occasionally used as a punishment for criminal casters.

"Surely the father then must have some say? Even given the situation," Janis argued. She'd heard the argument and felt it somewhat lacking. Obviously, there was a fact which was needed to connect the dots.

"The Father made the duel necessary," Platt said flatly.

Janis thought for a moment then opinioned. "He didn't want the child to enter any guild, did he? He felt overprotective perhaps?" Janis prodded.

"In simple terms, yes."

The larger picture was finally beginning to take shape. It was rare, though not unheard of, that a parent would refuse to allow their child to enter the guild system. Sometimes this mean the child would be brought up in a sort of underground, non-formalized method, or simply apprenticed to the parents in their own guild.

The fact that the father was not a powerful caster meant that the child may not receive proper training, and the guilds felt this was untenable based on the potential power level of the prospect. The duel seemed the best way to ensure that one of the guilds would have no interference from the others when it came time to legally challenge the father for the right to train the child.

Legal challenges like this were far from certain but generally went the way of the family. Janis only knew of a few cases where the parents' rights were overruled. These were extreme cases which usually revolved around the parents' incompetence or criminal tendencies. These things were very hard to prove in court.

The larger question came to Janis. Why had these duels resolved to death? Neither her nor my duels ended in murder. She asked the question more as an internal dialogue than as a direct interrogative.

When Platt answered she was almost startled out of her pensiveness.

"We never included an element of death being required. All of us undertook to keep the duels free from that potential, but I fear something else is happening which we were not prepared for. We have wondered but are bound by the magic to engage anyway. I suppose you being here is point in fact that some part of the spell must not affect you the way it did the original members of the casting conclave. Or that another force is working upon us during the duels, which had no effect on either you or your partner."

Janis was slightly taken back. She hadn't said anything about me. The fact that Platt was aware of both of them, meant that she had considerable resources attached to gathering information. Potentially part of the spell itself made that possible.

"We are both free now, and in both cases, there were no deaths involved. I think you might be more correct about the second point. As it turns out, I have had some knowledge about dueling and the rules associated to the tradition. The to the death component of the geas would have been built into the spell. I believe there is an outside force working toward these deaths."

Platt simply nodded.

"You have the names of the other gatherers I assume?" The Colonel asked. After Janis nodded, she continued. "I, myself, must soon engage in a duel I suggest you accompany me as my second, which is my right, and observe if there are other forces at work. Whatever they are they would need to be powerful enough to overcome our own innate compunction against killing. Further, it seems you and your partner are now free from continuing in the duel even though he won his duel, and you did not. Which means that either the original compulsion affected us differently than it did you, or, as you said, there is a greater outside influence than we suspect,"

"What do you think that means?" Janis prodded.

"I fear it means that someone or something has coopted the dueling spell and bound into it elements which we are unaware of and cannot detect. That can only mean that a very powerful or cunning caster is somehow involved."

No cure

Janis and I had returned to the station. The two guild police investigators were now attached to her at the hip. We'd commandeered one of the conference rooms and settled in for a long discussion on the case. Several new elements had come to light, and although we'd both been freed of our geas, we were beginning to feel like we were getting to the bottom of the case.

Having a list of those involved in the duels meant we should be able to at least track each person and do our best to intervene, before things took a turn for the worse. Our discussion centered on the idea that interrupting the duel without understanding the spell would invariably cause more harm than good, as these kind of geas often result in death or madness when ignored.

Janet wanted to understand the spell better in an attempt to create a counter spell to cure the duelists of the compulsion. To this end she spent an hour or so working on both her and me to discover the nature of the casting. As it turned out, I had no residual magical aura. For me, it was as though the spell had never been cast. Janis indicated this was due to my ability to dissemble.

When she used the same procedure on herself, she managed to understand the basic elements of the spell, but there were literally dozens of subcomponents which would take time to understand. Time was not a commodity we had in abundance.

Hastily, she composed a spell which she hoped would at least stifle the geas enough to allow each duelist to resist the killing urge, if this was indeed a component of the dueling spell. The detectives from the guild added a few elements to her effort to try and maximize its effect.

For myself, I began to understand the taste of the spell better. The acrid bitter sensation mixed with a sort of metalic and sickly-sweet undertone. There were lots of other flavors mixed in. This gave me the sense of a well-constructed entree, where each ingredient added to the flavor profile of the meal. There were textures and spices that simply overwhelmed my palate and masked the natural flavor of the spell.

I wanted to be more help but knowing that I didn't have the faintest idea what she was doing, and my own way of interpreting magic was far for scientific, left me with little to do but request that each of the gather duelists to be followed.

Janis had made the arrangement with Colonel Platt to be her second when the next duel came about, meant we would have a front row seat. Hopefully this would allow us to jam the spell up with Janis' counter spell.

As this was happening, I began to think through the events which we had determined led to the duel. A child with unknown abilities who was basically untrusted to use their abilities in a constructive way, was at the center of the case. So far, we had no information on the child. If we were to end the entire affair, we would need to understand its cause.

Now that there were watchful eyes on each of the duelists, and we'd done what we could as far as countering the spells effect, we sat in the conference room to talk over each element of the case.

I started the discussion with the point that had been playing on my mind.

“I might be easier if we knew who they were dueling over,” I insisted.

“The geas prevents them from telling,” Janis said. “But if the aspirant is as powerful as they indicate, there might be clues which could help us. We know it would have been at least a level five aspirant and that the child would have been born no more than ten years ago, as that would be within the timeframe for the child to have been apprenticed to one of the guilds.”

“I can go through all the birth records and see if there are any children meeting that description,” I offered. “But that assumes that their birth was recorded. Although it is normal to do so, I can see a few reasons the parents would not do that, especially if the child is as powerful as each of these gatherers seems to think. Still, it can’t hurt.”

I stepped over to the reader which stood in a corner of the room and began going through the library of records. I listened to the conversation while I worked, hoping to pick up on other clues as they talked things out.

Detective Drakkin offered the idea that they could also check on the history of the father if they used some of the clues to who he was. I was asked to add a list of possible births, deaths and employment records for the suggested period of time, increasing the workload and making me feel slightly like a secretary.

I knew that the other investigators viewed me as being a sort of second left foot. It goes with the territory, and I've managed to get over my feelings of inadequacy more than once. Janis never made me feel that way, so I worked hard to not care what other casters thought of me.

The flow of the conversation moved back and forth on both the casters and the basic construct of a dueling spell. I was still more than a little surprised to discover that Janis had some experience in this area. I resolved to ask her more about it when I had the chance.

I knew very little of her personal life. It had not ever really occurred to me to ask. She rarely talked about her past and it just seemed to me to be part of the cost of being partnered with a caster. This time, I felt it would be nice to know more about her. Curiosity is a required component of being a detective.

But there is also an unspoken agreement to not pry too much. Each of us has a life outside of work. No matter how well or closely we work together, our real life has nothing to do with work. That is until it does have something to do with work. Maybe this was one of those times.

As I worked, I tried to listen in on the conversation, but so much magically technical discussion was going on that I could hardly follow. Sometimes listening to her is like trying to decipher another language. I suppose that is a reality for any highly specialized profession. Half of learning the trade is learning what all the terminology means.

Even with my specialized training I'd received to join the magical crimes division, I could only follow about a tenth of the conversation.

Most of it was on the structure of the counter spell they planned on deploying. Janis was building the components. Creating a spell this complex took a lot of time and energy though. At this point she could only make a plan on how to construct it.

Spells with this much complexity cannot be cast quickly, but the actual timing of them activating can be controlled by any number of techniques. By that, I mean a spell can be sort of charged up then released when needed, with a few words or gestures in combination, or stored in an object or “focus”. That is how most “on the spot” casting actually happens.

I guess I should maybe go into more detail for those of you who read this and don’t really know how it works. If you are an experienced caster, then you should just jump past my rather remedial description.

There are several levels of spells which can take from a few seconds to several days or more to cast. The quick ones are usually referred to as “flicks”. Generally, they have either a simple effect, such as starting a fire or opening a door. Because they are easy to do, you can generally put a decent level of power in the spell. Most spells take much more time to cast. These can be charged into a focus or held back waiting for the activation element to take effect. These are referred to as “casts” or “castings”.

The caster constructs them with components similar to building a sentence. An effect, power, and a triggering component are the minimal requirements. Some spells are more complex and have things like adverbs and adjectives to specify not just a general effect, but a very specific set of effects. Maybe even a specific sequence of effects. You may even include a preloaded level of power. Obviously the more complex the effect, the longer the spell takes to cast. Having a trigger is still a requirement.

When a spell is imbued into an object, the trigger might be simply pointing the item at the target and thinking about the effect. This is how many magical fire-starters work.

When a spell is held back, it is basically stored in the back of the casters mind or the focus till the trigger activates the spell. High level casters can have dozens of spells ready to activate.

Often, a practitioner will have several items with spells built into them. These magical items are sort of like a purse for magic which can be opened to find the spell you need. In fact, there is a whole line of just that, magical purses, which go for a premium at the specialty shops. Also available is a variety of wallets and bag of tricks line.

Some items can be used by non-casters. They can take pretty much any shape and have almost any effect. The limitation is that whatever the effect, it cannot be altered in any way unless by a caster.

A decent caster can use an imbued object and subtly alter effect, range, power level and so on, while triggering the object. Whereas, a non-caster cannot.

This is all an oversimplification of course, but I think you get the point.

The other thing you should know is that casters are generally separated into groups based on power level. If a caster is above level two, they have to have a special registration. Level one and two are the lower levels, and most casters in these categories can hold back maybe four or five low level spells. None of the spells cast by these levels are very powerful, unless they use an outside source of magical power.

Level three casters make up the majority of the magical community. At this level a person may hold more than a dozen spells in reserve, and even be capable of imbuing an object. Also, they are able to cast a wider variety of spells than the lower power levels. It takes more training and focus to use the higher levels so their "vocabulary" of spell components must be larger.

I knew that Janis was a level four caster. These are very rare. Only maybe one in a thousand are capable of casting at this level. Highly dynamic and powerful spells are available and perhaps two dozen or more spells can be held in reserve. Level four is also the level at which a caster can begin to differentiate the way a spell was cast and not just the effect. Janis had also shown that she could sometimes tell exactly who cast a spell based on how it was constructed. Janis was even capable of creating reasonably powerful and detailed spells on the fly.

Only three level five casters were known to live, currently. These casters are the pinnacle of magical ability and have been known to create castings of highly complex nature from their imaginations, as well as having access to essentially unlimited magical power. All of the living fives were heads of the international orders for their guild. I can't remember the others, but one of them is an Aresinia.

Janis was thinking on how to build the spell she would require. It could take time to create, which we might not have. Still, it was important to do everything we could to thwart the dueling ring so that no one else would die.

I thought of another point that they all seemed reluctant to discuss. Some spells can be disentangled by attacking certain components of the spell construct. But that could only happen if you had intrinsic knowledge of the construction of the spell.

I suppose the final thought I had was that I might be able to break the spell by dissembling it. I had the suspicion that they wanted to avoid that eventuality. Perhaps they felt that it would be some sort of insult that a dud could have any kind of control over a powerful caster.

I found the files I was looking for and copied them to the paper folder. Then I walked back over to the conference table and made a slight "humphing" sound to get the attention of my collogues.

"Looks like about a dozen births in that timeframe that might fit the bill. I went ahead and checked to see if any were already apprenticed to any of the guilds and found that half of them were. The remaining seven run the gamut between super wealthy and poor as dirt. But two look really promising. One being a middle class caster whose son was designated with a form of hyperfocus known as Crelins Syndrome. This seems to be a learning disorder when the person has trouble shifting focus from one thing to another, sometimes fixating for days, or even weeks, on a single thing," I informed them.

"The other has a form of autism which seems to occur only in casters. It presents as a sort of inability to understand or connect with other people. I suspect that both would have been part of the special needs gatherers effort. And I also suspect that hyperfocus or autism might be considered challenging if the potential had an unusually high-power level."

"Okay, so those are the known potentials who might be at the center of the dueling circle," Janis nodded. "Did you find anything which might indicate another possibility? Say, someone who was not tested at birth? Maybe a rich family where the births were private and only recorded in the national register of births?"

"Well," I paused. "That is harder to connect. I made some assumptions and found a few more of the wealthier families with some influence in the Caster community which might be possibilities, but all of these children except one have been gathered into one of the guilds. The one remaining in this category seems to have fallen off the face of the earth.

There are no additional medical records or school records, really nothing to show that the child existed except their birth registration."

"So, in all there are three," Detective Norvorst seemed pleased. "We can trace each one of them in pretty short order, I think."

"Shall we split up then and check each out?" I offered.

We were interrupted by a desk Sergeant who insisted she had important information for us. There had been another murder. This time the magical duel had been committed in a public place, and there were several witnesses.

The two antagonists stood some twenty feet apart. One seemed confident while the other was trembling. A casual observer would have thought the tall man was nervous and the rather slight woman to be almost arrogant.

Neither was true. The quaking joints of the man were due to his level of adrenaline enhancing his naturally compressed personality. And the woman, though outwardly calm, could barely contain her anticipation.

A crowd had gathered thinking that this was some planned display of magic which sometimes occurred as a way of creating interest and common goodwill between the casting community and the non-casters. These things were often seen as a sort of fireworks display combined with a historical reenactment.

Dueling had at one time been very common. And like the old-west shows creatively reliving the famous gun battles in the wild west, a duel such as this seemed more entertainment than real.

The thin pale man looked as though he were on the verge of falling over. His frame was so slight that he seemed to be starved. Although he appeared to be very old, he was actually only in his late thirties.

The woman was also thin, but in her case, it seemed that this was due to her taking care of herself. She was completely composed and calm. Her eyes were sharp and clear and the slight smile that crossed her face was both pleasant and at the same time sort of terrifying. She seemed young but was actually in her late fifties.

The man flicked his wrist and spoke a word in an archaic form of Latin. A dead language for a Necromage seemed almost too pretentious. A whisp of air flowed around him. Faces formed in the mist which rose from the pavement at his feet.

The woman stepped back with her left foot and reached into a deep pocket in her long trench coat. The object she retrieved was a long cylinder about 2 inches in diameter and six inches long.

She held it up in front of her and shook it once. A rainbow of light erupted from it and flowed from her to the Necromage in slow waves. The mist, which had been building, recoiled when the multicolored light touched it.

After a slight retreat the mist stopped, then firmed up, then began to push against the waves of light. Where the light and the mist touched a line of black negative energy sparked.

It was along this interface of energy that the duel was being fought. Each combatant pushed more power into their spell. The intensity of interaction along the frontier increased.

The Necromage added an element of intricacy known as a "daemon stare". This component was generally used to draw life energy from the victim.

The Technomage responded by pulling on one end of the tube. With a twist, she activated a power reserve to counter the life force drain. She was aware that the power would be used up quickly as it had been stored in the talisman like a battery. This also meant her rainbow attack would be limited in duration.

She would have to end the duel quickly or turn to another attack. She decided on the latter and rapidly spun on her heal and clicked the toe of her left shoe to the concrete. A flick of lightning erupted from the crack in the ground she'd just made.

The lightning and accompanying thunder struck at her opponent and threw him off balance.

She spun and clicked again, and again.

The Necromage staggered backward with each blast. He was clearly unprepared for the attack. He desperately wove his arms to create an ad hoc defensive Flick known as the "Styx Defense". This spell was basically a high-power, low complexity, magical shield.

Unfortunately for him, the lightning itself was not magical in nature. Though generated from a magical device, the static charge was a result of magical crystals touching off on the concrete. This was directed by the Talismantecha by her expert spin and kicking action.

The Necromage fell to the ground in a heap. Sweat poured from his brow and his already ghostly pallor became whiter, and his face seemed too thin to the point of becoming skeletal. His eyes glazed over.

All of the action took less than thirty seconds, during which the crowd stood looking on, entertained by the magical display.

A loud round of applause followed the event as an officer stepped forward. His hands were out in a gesture of appeasement. It was clear he too thought this was a street performance. However, these things were always preceded by showing a display permit to a local officer and having them standing by during the event in case of need.

The Talismantecha stepped toward the officer and held out her hands in a sign of capitulation.

"Where is your permit?" he asked.

“I surrender myself to your custody for formal charges of dueling and murder,” she replied.

The officer stood there in awe for several moments before he decided she was being serious. He quickly ran to the defeated Necromage and checked him out. After determining that she had indeed killed him, he returned to her and offered the obligatory reading of rights and cuffed her.

Janis and I arrived on the scene only ten minutes later.

Donna Brackenshith had been read her rights and condescended to our impromptu interview without a lawyer. Janis was well aware that she would only divulge in formation by way of confirmation of facts already known. Because of this the interview was short. Janis did, however, discover some new information by implying that we already knew a few facts which were merely theories before.

When questioning the Talismantecha gatherer Janis used the name of the child whose birth had been recorded but had no other records.

"Tell us how you intended to gather the child Millen BenDarvin?" She asked in a curt and clear tone.

"I planned on winning the duels," she said in a soft tone. "But I did not intend to kill."

"You did kill," Janis said abruptly. "You didn't have too, but you did."

"No. I tried to limit the amount of energy in each of my attacks, but somehow, I could not control myself. I could feel the urge, the temptation to utterly destroy him and I could not resist," she sighed. "I may have underestimated, or even misunderstood, the nature of this challenge. I know I must pay the price. I did not want to kill him."

"I want you to tell me everything you know about the dueling spell," Janis ordered.

"I can't, there is a binding which prevents me from saying. Even though I want to tell you something important, which I think would help, I cannot bring myself to tell you. The compulsion is very strong," she replied.

Janis sighed and stepped back. She leaned toward me and asked me a somewhat confusing question.

“If I guide you through it, we might be able to dissemble the dueling spell and allow her to be free from the compulsion, but also from the effects of the duel. Are you willing to try?”

“Sure, I guess.”

“You have to be careful not to do too much. If I just let you go unchecked you might accidentally damage her innate magical abilities.”

“Wait. Is this dangerous?” I asked.

“I don’t know. This is not something I think has ever been done before. When working with magic experimentally unexpected things can happen. What I want to do is coach both of you so that only the dueling spell is affected, but really, I don’t know?”

“We should ask her permission first,” I said.

Janis nodded and stepped back toward Brackenshith. “Donna, my associate is skilled at understanding the nature of various spells.

I'd like to try to make more sense of this by trying a little experiment. I want you to understand there might be a danger which we cannot predict in this experiment. Do you give us permission to proceed?"

A worried look accompanied her response of "yes."

At the station we commandeered an interview room. I sat across from Janis and Donna, and a member of the Order of Hermes stood attendance in the adjoining room watching through the large picture window.

My senses were already tingling and even before Janis began the experiment I began to shuffle through the variety of tastes and smells from the magic, which exuded from our interviewee.

I recognized the flavor of the spell. It was a complex combination of spices and other less palatable tastes. The overlaying cloy was that of honey mixed with a salty element, which seemed to both enhance and ruin the flavor.

Janis was slowly instructing the Talismantecha duelist to try to explain any portion of the duel rules. This amounted to a breach of the geas and would therefore cause a strain on her. She would not be able to actually betray the duelists, but by creating the effort, she might reveal the elements of the spell used and allow me to dissemble them.

A small line of sweat began to raise across her brow. To me, the air was filled with an overwhelming scent of milk and sugar with a sort of malty or grainy texture thrown in. I separated the sweetness and the milk and saw the thread in them which could be severed and did so. That left only the malted grain. I could taste several lines of flavor winging back through the more complex spell. and felt myself being drawn toward a particularly offensive sensation which grew in intensity, till all the other elements seemed drowned out. I could feel how intrinsically this was connected to all the other flavors and smells.

“Janis,” I said, “There is an overwhelming element here connected to everything, almost making it impossible to know where one piece begins and another ends.”

“I think you have found the source of her power,” you need to back off and try to sense the spell. I’ll prompt her again to try even harder. Find the most obvious thread not the most powerful.”

“Not sure that makes sense but…” I replied.

As Janis again instructed Brackenshith, I tasted the thread of malted grain and recognized the flavor of children's cereal. It seemed an odd but obvious interpretation of the spell, and I saw not only how powerful it was, but also how complex. There was a nut accent and undertones of corn and wheat, as well as some kind of dried fruit, which I took for sugared dates.

I searched for all the connections within this particular flavor profile and severed them. Again, the powerful offensive odor returned in full force. I could see that all the connections and intertwining threads from this flavor would be easy to cut and found myself, without thinking, beginning to sever one of the smallest. A scream broke my concentration, and as my mind returned fully to consciousness, I saw Janis bending over the slumping form of the talismantecha. Her face was ashen and she seemed unnerved.

The effort had drained me completely. I passed out in exhaustion.

Janis was gently slapping my face and calling my name softly. I awoke still spent from the effort. I startled as I remembered the scream.

"What happened?" I asked.

"You did take the spell apart quite effectively. She has been talking for the better part of the last half hour. I let you rest a little bit," Janis said quietly.

"Is she okay?"

"She will be fine. You almost caused a pretty big stir though."

"Why?"

"Jack," she paused and thought over how to tell me something which was obviously both important and also evidently somewhat delicate.

"Jack, you almost magically lobotomized her."

"What!" I did not even try to hide my surprise.

"The overpowering deep and central element which you sensed was her power node. Essentially the place where she draws her magic from. Without this, she would be cut off from that source and no amount of healing could give her the ability to use magic again."

"I didn't think that was possible," I sighed.

"Jack, there are secret histories within the guilds which I should not tell you, but now that you are coming to be aware of your own abilities it is important to explain this so you understand your role."

She paused again, gathering the words and formatting her information. I knew I was about to have a college lecture on some magical history, and that I probably would only understand half of what she would tell me.

"In the past, during the first guild war, a war which lasted nearly six hundred years, it was decided that only by truly enforcing our strictures against certain uses of magic, could we codify the guilds and build a future with the non-casting people. Wars had devastated the world and left a barren wasteland barely habitable. The population of the world had plummeted to extinction levels.

"A child was born who changed the world. Not by what she built, but by what she could destroy. She was the first recorded dissembler. As the final battles raged, she walked untouched through the fires and storms of magical power. With a thought, she broke the magic and left the fields silent. Then when she herself was attacked by one of the most powerful casters of the war, she simply took apart his magic.

“It was fear that stopped the wars. This deep need for self-preservation extended to the preservation of each casters magical abilities. Without magic they would be normal non-casters, and, in their minds, lesser humans.

“For many centuries after the war, people like you were used as final punishment for magical crimes. The thought of using a dissembler kept the levels of magical crime very low.

“It was the first compact between Normals and Casters that changed all the ideas that normal society had about individual rights, which began to be seen as desirable in the caster legal system.The idea of terminating someone's magical abilities was seenas cruel and unusual, and finally outlawed. In the end, everyone who had this ability was marginalized, and we even stopped looking for those with the ability.

“The first sign of this power is the ability to sense, but not actually construct, magical spells. Many who have this ability don’t even know it. Only perhaps one percent can actually discern the properties of a spell enough to take it apart. That said, it is possible that any person who is a dud could potentially be a dissembler. At least on a small scale.

“It was not until I started working with you that I realized how strong your ability was, and the potential for you to use it. It is still a sort of casters dirty secret, so it is not discussed. The histories is very clear though, about how intrinsic a person like you would have been in society two thousand years ago. You would have been the royal executioner of the day, respected, but shunned. More powerful than the most powerful caster, because with a force of will, you could render anyone powerless.

“It was only your natural instinct against harming people that stopped you from completely severing Brackenshith’s power center and rendering a final judgment for her illegal use of magic. The thing is, that the old laws still hold sway. You have the right to act as judge and jury. You could have legally and rightfully punished her for her transgression."

"You're saying that an archaic tradition like that hasn't been stricken. Its barbaric." I interjected.

"Yes, it is, and yet we have never rescinded the rule. It was placed for a reason. Even though times have changed, the alure of power is still a problem, especially among those in power. Some are not content with their place in the world, however elevated. The distance between using your power to help the world, and craving more and more power, is often razon thin. Among non-casters there is always a ceiling which keeps your people from rising above ours. You use technology to advance your cause, and we use magic. If both cannot be proportionately distributed, equality cannot be achieved. Everyone has to have a say in the future, otherwise those who would try to build their power to control and pursue their own goals will win," she was lecturing again.

I know it is not because she thinks of me as of lower intelligence or anything, so I tried not to take it personally. In this case though, I felt somewhat like a first grader talking to a professor of whatever.

"Jack," she continued. "As of now, you are the most powerful person around. You need to learn to use this new found ability and use it wisely. I would like to help."

"Yes, you are right," I felt more confident now.

"It is what I wanted all along. As I said, I thought you might have this power from the beginning. It was why I wanted to be partnered with you. I'll tell you this one last secret between us. I studied dissemblers and the laws surrounding them at my guild. I have always been fascinated by the idea that there might be a way to control, even by fear, the casters who might use their abilities for crime. It has been a long time coming for us to return to the older ways. We have become too powerful and assured of our supremacy. Casters need to have something to fear."

In the pit, we gathered the team of investigators who had been working on the case. The three detectives from the guilds, Janis, and I took the central table in the room and set to planning our next steps. As the rest of the office consisted of the other two magical crime teams from the Seattle office, we were free to discuss everything freely and also included them.

When we told them that the duel was not originally meant to be to the death, and the compulsion to participate, everyone focused on the new question of how that particular set of features had been insinuated into the spell.

Detective Drakkin was of the opinion that we should simply arrest all the involved parties now that they were known and keep them in separate cells till the time limit ran out.

Janis squashed that idea quickly by reminding everyone that the geas of the duel was so strong it would possibly kill any of the gatherers that refused or were prevented from carrying it out.

We hadn't told any of the investigators about my status as a dissembler yet. Only Janis and the member of the Order of Hermes, who had witnessed the interview earlier, knew what I could do.

"Either way, I think that the end game will be dueling and endangerment, but the actual murders end up being tossed by reason of influence by magical curse. In reality, none of them will probably face more than what amounts to a slap on the wrist," Detective Dramont acknowledged.

"I suppose the extenuating circumstance of the powerful prospect was enough to incite this particular series of events. Legally or otherwise, I think that they might all be judged as complicit, but not actually responsible," Janis agreed.

"It leaves us with the same question, what next?" I asked.

"I think the two of you should interview the BenDarvin's," Norvorst insisted. "We can keep an eye on the rest of the duelists to make sure no one gets killed. Everything considered, it's probably not going to get solved unless we get to the root, and the root seems to be the Child."

Everyone agreed we should make contact, so we found the address and did a contact call to validate they would be at home. Once we ascertained we could have a personal interview, Janis and I headed to the judicial desk to get an interview warrant and a continuing investigation certificate. After which we headed to the home of the BenDarvin's.

It was a stately home on Mercer Island near the north point on Lake Washington. The closest home was roughly a quarter mile south of the gated main drive. The estate was named after the neighborhood, which had once stood in the area. A large wrought iron sign declared the Roanoke Estate.

We range in at the gate where a pretty standard talisman gate opener kept the grounds secure. After advertising our bona fides the gates swung open, and we drove the 500 yards up the drive to the main house.

An elderly man waited at the steps to escort us to the master of the estate. He was obviously a non-caster butler, hearkening back to a tradition of servitude by the less powerful to those with either money or power. I felt somewhat incensed, but kept my feelings in check.

Janis and I found ourselves deposited in an ornate living room where antique furniture and opulent affectations adorned every exposed surface. The overall impression was that of someone desperately trying to show off their status. To say it was a vulgar display of wealth would be an understatement. It was nearly a half hour before the lanky, and somewhat sinister looking, Mr. BenDarvin decided to join us.

The somewhat patented "How can I help the fine police establishment?" was not only obviously offensive, but downright smug. He finished with, "I am not generally in the habit of contributing to the Police Magical League, but I will make an exception."

"Actually, we are here on a case," Janis informed him perfunctorily. She handed him the writ of warrant. "We are aware that you and your son are the subjects of a duel for the right to mentor him at whichever guild wins." She paused to see if he would respond. He didn't.

"We are going to ask you a few questions. Do you feel you need to have an attorney present?"

His brow furrowed slightly as though he were upset. Quickly, he returned to the imperturbable expressions of superiority. "That depends on the questions. Please sit."

I almost felt like I was offending the gods by sitting in a chair which was obviously worth more than my own home. The sentiment of caution overwhelmed me. I found myself hoping my hands weren't dirty. I crossed them in my lap to avoid tarnishing the ornately carved arms.

As I sat, I began to taste the aura of magic which surrounded almost every object. A familiar pepper and bile reminded me of the dueling chamber. I was sure there was a connection. My mind raced with the thought that perhaps he, Mr. BenDarvin, had been the architect of the stray components of the spell.

I realized quickly that I was only conjecturing, and even with the similar signatures of power and context, we would not be able to prove he had any involvement, other than insisting the duel be fought.

“We have information that you initiated a duel between various gatherers for the tutoring of your child in one of the guilds. Is that true?” Janis asked directly.

“Duel? No. I simple informed them that I was not interested in the machinations of any particular guild and would not hear any plea about my son until they themselves had determined who would represent the magical community. I believe I was joking when I said something like, and I cannot be sure if it was exactly this, you may duel for his allegiance for all I care.”

“So, you are saying the duels which have now claimed several lives are nothing more than a misunderstanding about an offhand remark you made?” Janis continued to press.

“I don’t know. Who can know for sure why they all decided to go this route. I was unaware of the fact they were dueling until you told me a few moments ago. Last I'd heard from any of them was yesterday when Dr. Fromale called to say someone would contact me within two days about the disposition of the guilds toward my son."

"What is your area of magical expertise?"

"I wouldn't call myself an expert. I'm a relatively low level caster in the Aresinia. My specialty, if you can call it that, is non-intrusive surveillance."

"Military intelligence?" Janis prompted.

"Yes," he smiled. "I'm afraid I cannot tell you more than that, as some of my work is considered classified."

"Of course," Janis returned his smile. "Why did you not just send your son to the Aresinia?"

"He is very powerful. I was not sure the warriors would offer the best education for him. I have no particular loyalty to Aresinia, other than my own membership. My hope for my son is that he rises above any particular familial restrictions or loyalties and find his own path."

“The boy's mother?”

“What about her?” he retorted somewhat offended. “She died during childbirth. I’ve done all I can to make his life good. I’ve even foregone any romantic entanglements to make sure he has everything he needs. I live for my son, and I won’t have just anyone take him from me. When the guilds prove who is worthy of his membership, I’ll step aside and give them my full measure of thanks.”

His comment seemed to allude to something deeper and I hoped Janis would get him to expound, but she slid in a different direction.

“She was a member of the Order of Hermes?”

“Yes,” his calm seemed to return. “She was a talented physician. Her place as the Head of Medicine at University Hospital, and her family money, paid for all this. I would never have been able to attain this kind of wealth. Not to say I did not have my own resources from my family, but they were nothing like that which her family had obtained.”

“Do you mind me asking where her family got its wealth?” Janis continued down what I was starting to consider a useless path.

"The old days. Her family were from the old Longinus line. Some of the most influential and powerful casters in history. Most belonged to Aresinia. I think she defied them when she chose Hermes," his smile of pride seemed genuine. "Maybe she chose me to marry as a further insult to them. I was never very powerful. Perhaps I might have become an officer if I showed my tenacity or skill, but probably not. As a level 2 I would never achieve much. I focused on castings that were simple and effective with not much power required. In fact, the less power used was sometimes the better, as the castings are harder to detect. Somewhat more insidious." His smile turned into a sneer.

I could tell he was gloating. He seemed to be a perfect example of a person who tastes a little power and craves more. Like a drug which he had become addicted too. A little was never enough.

"How old is your son?"

"Millen is ten," He replied.

"Normally a child is inducted to a guild by the age of seven. Why did you wait this long?"

“Simply put, Millen has trouble interacting with others. I felt it would be better if he matured a little. To give him more social skill. He is powerful enough that he could do harm or cause problems
if unable to integrate into the guild system.”

“How were you going to help him integrate?”

“I’ve been helping him interact with more and more individuals and small groups, both of friendly people which are familiar, and new faces which will hopefully give him a feeling of security and belonging. I admit I made the mistake of being his only human contact for much of his childhood. This left him somewhat remedial in his social abilities.”

“Can we meet him?” Janis seemed more insistent than the words implied.

“I will arrange it,but not right now. He has been somewhat disturbed of late. He sometimes has moments of aggression which can last several hours. During these times, I have him stay in a magically secured room where his power cannot affect anyone accidentally.”

“Very thoughtful,” Janis nodded. “If you can contact us when he can be available, we would be grateful. We only want to ask him a couple of questions. You have the right to refuse, of course, as his parent,” she was obviously offering him a way out. Either way he didn’t bite.

“I am sure he will feel better by this evening. Say after dinner. 8 pm will be a good time,” he replied. “Will there be anything else?”

“Just one thing, does your work for Aresinia ever include piggybacking spells?”

He seemed startled for a moment, then became as implacable as before. “I cannot, of course, tell you if my duties included anything like that. Also, piggybacking spells is not looked upon as being particularly honorable. Somewhat gutter magic if you ask me.”

Complex and Simple

We returned to the station and called the team back together. With a little more information, and what seemed to be a strong hunch carried by Janis, we reviewed the clues.

"I would like to recreate the spell," Janis said. "On paper anyway. It doesn't need to be particularly accurate, we only need to have an idea of how it was done so we can counter it," she paused as though she were considering what to say.

"Some of you know that Jack is a dud. He cannot cast, but he can sense magic. It turns out he is also a dissembler. If we find the proper linchpin in the dueling spell, we can make it safe. Essentially removing the geas, and hopefully discovering how the spell was cast and who is responsible for adding the deadly features."

The silence was thick. Everyone in the room looked at me with fear and wonder. For my part, I began to feel uncomfortable at the quiet, and I offered a thought.

"My goal will be to take out the parts of the spell which are causing the problems, and nothing more. I am aware of the potential problems, so I need as much information as I can get to make sure I do only that."

"So let us build the spell as though we were second years initiates. We'll start with effect and power. Then add supplemental components. Just like writing a sentence. Although, I think this one might be considered a run on," her joke was missed by everyone except me who knew her too well to let it pass.

"And on and on and on," I added.

That broke the silence. The team got to work thinking through how the spell needed to be constructed. It became clear that the spell would be powered by each of the participants as they completed the circuiting ritual in the dueling chamber. With that component out of the way, we got down to the specific effects and how they might be constructed.

To be sure, I didn't help that much. It was the casters who worked through this exercise. All I did was listen and make sure I understood as much as I could, so I might be able to recognize the components when I sensed them.

"A list of the main effects will include the urge to duel, a time limit, and several components for drawing the power the spell needs to bind each participant. I feel like there might not have been a definition for what constituted a victory which might have enabled the piggyback of dueling to the death," Norvorst was saying.

"Probably, it was meant to follow the old dueling tradition where a person could admit defeat. That would account for you being free after your run in with Colonel Platt," Dremont added.

"I think that makes sense," Janis added. "But I think that the particular part of the geas was specific to the gatherers because I never felt the continuing urge to kill. Is it possible that the piggyback of death was only in effect for a small period of time during the initial casting? If it were powered by a low level caster, it might have faded before the main effect of the spell."

“That makes more sense,” Dremont agreed. “You obviously have someone in mind.”

“The father is the most likely candidate,” Janis nodded.

“Okay so let's say he added this effect himself, how would that effect have not been known by the duelists?”

“There are really two spells here,” Janis explained. “One for the duel and one for the dueling space. The extra dimensional location which had to be navigated in order to have the actual spell cast. The same group of casters would have been responsible for building that location, and it was probably within that casting that the subtle part of the casting occurred. I think

BenDarvin knows about piggybacking and I think that he might be really good at it. I can’t prove it, but I’m pretty sure.”

“So, are we looking at decifering the dueling spell or the location creation spell?” Norvorst asked.

"Still both," Janis replied. "They are intertwined spells. One draws from the other."

"I think the general outline of the spells works like this," she paused to collect her thoughts. "Once it was decided to duel for the right to gather Millen BenDarvin, the gatherers planned to use the old tradition of a gathering place which would infuse the spell. They planned the spell as a group, and even passed the components each added from one to the next, so that the combined spell would be organized correctly."

"BenDarvin looked for places in each of the spells to cast a part of the death geas. Each would have been innocuous by itself but one combined after the actual casting of the dueling spell, the measure would have been in full force, powered originally by BenDarvin, but sustained in power by the individual duelists."

"We, Jack and I, didn't traverse the original spell till after the effect added by BenDarvin faded, so we were not under the same geas to kill. Also, Colonel Platt didn't feel the geas to kill me."

"All that makes sense. I think the thing then, is to find the linchpins, as you said, and make sure Detective Cadance knows how to pull them." Drakkin seemed to finally be getting into the spirit of the thing.

"I wonder at the reason though?" I asked. "I mean why would someone go to all the effort to do this. To potentially kill so many people. What is the motive?"

"Perhaps if we discover the motive then we discover the murderer," Janis said succinctly.

"All right. Let's look at it from that angle. Why would anyone want these people to go to that extreme?" I asked.

"I hate to be the bearer of bad tidings, but it might be no more complex than the person responsible was a traditionalist. Duels to the death were an ancient way of determining things like this. Admittedly, the practice was abandoned long before the modern guild system. Still, it could be the basis for a motive," Norvorst theorized.

"Seems to me another potential motive might be a little hidden. Perhaps the duel was a ruse to have one particular gatherer killed. Maybe some old grudge?" I thought aloud.

"Or maybe a stab at the heart of the system. Our guild system is thought by some to be restrictive and overburdening. Maybe the underground or someone with sympathies that way?" Drakkin added.

"It's a good thought, but everyone involved is pretty ingrained in the system. I think we keep it on the list, but it's not at the top," Norvorst replied.

"Whatever the motive, the fact remains we have a limited number of suspects. These being the remaining gatherers, and if Janis is right, it's the father," I said. "If we look at each of them in turn, we might figure this out."

"Okay. Let's start with Colonel Platt. She would want the power that comes from having the child. Or to make sure that power did not end up in any other guild. As an Aresinia, she would have knowledge of the proper spell constructs and piggybacks. She might also have been immune to the effect, which could explain why she didn't kill you Janis," Drakkin chimed in again.

"In a way, each of the gatherers could have the same motive, but it would be highly unlikely that any, except Dr. Fromale or The Colonel, would have the knowledge on how to make it happen," Dremont added.

"If it were Dr. Fromale, we'd have a hard time tracing it since he is dead. But I agree he should be on the list. But you bring up a good point Drakkin. Motive gets us nowhere without means. In this case, means includes the ability to cast certain types of spells, which we are for now assuming are piggybacks on the dueling setup," Janis mused. "That means we really only have a list of three. Dr. Fromale, Colonel Platt, and Mr. BenDarvin."

"What would be BenDarvin's motive?" I asked.

We paused, each searching their thoughts and experience for the answer. It came to me as it came to the others, and it came to all of us at nearly the same instant. I cannot say for certain who said it first, but it felt like a chorus when we all blurted out, “His son.”

Millen BenDarvin was born mid-summer on a hot and muggy day. His mother had been in labor for hours. A midwife from the Order of Hermes stood vigil as she went from an almost catatonic state of relaxation to the most vigorously painful convulsions.

The father had been called home from work. He felt not only love and affection for his wife, but also a deep sense of gratitude for having chosen him to love and marry. Their few years together had been the most fulfilling and rewarding he'd ever known. Now he knew that his life was going to change and that they would share a child. Together they would make the world a better place as a family. Maybe they'd have more children. He was in elation as he drove home that morning.

He ran up the stairs taking three at a time. The shouts died out by the time he flung open the door to the birthing suite. A soft sob accompanied the soft cries of the baby.

The room was in turmoil. Red stains and splatters washed the walls and ceiling in a dreadful artwork. The baby was in the arms of the midwife crying softly. The midwife wept as she stood near the end of the bed obscuring the scene beyond. There was nothing recognizable in the bed. No hint that the body there had once been a beautiful young woman. The mangled corpse was no longer articulated, and each bone seemed to have been shattered. The sight of the bloody pulp caused Torrey BenDarvin to retch. He didn't notice the soft glow of power from his newborn son.

Janis and I arrived at the BenDarvin home at 5 minutes before eight. Time for the duels was running out, and although we'd kept watch on the remaining duelists, no other activity had compromised our afternoon of musing.

Again, we were escorted into the opulent living room. We sat and waited for our presence to be acknowledged. It was several minutes later that the father escorted his son in.

The taste of pepper and bile was suddenly overwhelming.

In our previous meeting here, I assumed it came from the father and indeed there was some element of it in him, now, however, I knew that this originated with the son.

The boy was small for his age. The overlarge head was mostly from the eyes up. An almost egg-shaped cranium topped a frame that was so fragile the boy seemed like he might topple over. Like his father, he wore an expensive tailored three-piece suit of dark gray. His black eyes were piercing and matched his jet-black hair. The boy looked a lot like his father with the exception of the goatee his father wore.

I wasn't sure if Janis knew, but I did as soon as I met the child. He was as evil a child as ever had been. He probed with his eyes into my mind, and I tasted the spell as it hit me.

I reactively split it and broke its construction. I was not really aware of how the components worked, but the spell was powerful.

I followed the trail of the spell and found the child had used the exact construct on Janis. She was not immune and turned on me in an instant and began a complex casting.

I'd seen this spell before. It was a combat spell, and it was deadly. Instead of focusing on her I fought to break apart the spell he was using on her.

I felt for and found the pepper element and turned it off. Janis slumped and sighed. Then turned to the boy and began to set up some defenses.

The child did not hesitate to press the attack. Another wave of very powerful force ran toward both of us. These were more difficult to unentangle. The child was using some highly complex magic for someone not yet initiated into the racks of the guild system.

If I would have guessed in the moment, I'd have thought this was due to his father's teaching him. Since his father was somewhat less powerful, he relied on more complex spells to achieve his goals. In any case, the spell was beginning to work on us again before I dissembled it.

Each of these spells were a different kind of mental control. I didn't have the expertise to know the difference, but I could tell what was being attempted. I could also tell that Millen was pushing another spell. Unless I took drastic action, Janis and I would eventually fall before the powerful onslaught.

I reached out to the spell and past the spell. I found the intertwining waves and threads of the magical construct. Here, unlike in the few others, was such complexity and power, that I could hardly tell one element from another.

I grasped at a thread and pulled. The taste of it made me sick. This was tied, or connected in some way, to several other threads of power. Each seemed to add a level of nausea as I separated them from the first thread. After clipping away a dozen other threads it was free. And the main part of the tangle remained. So, I grasped another thread and started again.

There was a point at which I stopped thinking in terms of this thread and that wave. I don't remember how it happened, and my idea of time was somewhat skewed by the rapidity at which events around me transpired.

The truth is, my focus was so complete that my mind did not register anything other than my effort to take apart the massively powerful attack which had been unleashed.

I suppose, in retrospect, that a certain awareness of the truth came to me during this time, and I'll share that with you later. But mostly I was occupied by the seemingly insurmountable task of tearing down the spell which was attacking me and my partner.

Although I don't expect anyone to really understand it, and even I who was performing this task don't, I am going to attempt to describe the effort in the hope that I can refer to it later.

Threads and waves are in themselves nothing. They are but conduits for magical intent. The threads are ways of transferring power, and the waves are a sort of force behind the spell. I'm probably just confusing you, but I realize now that creation of a spell requires will, structure, and power. If any of these things are missing, the spell simply cannot work.

The waves are a representation of will. You see all of these impressions are my own interpretation of the magic which was attacking me. I've come to use these metaphors as my model by which I do what I do.

So, then threads are conduits constructed by the structure of the spell, and waves are the intent or will of the caster. Finally, there must be a power source, a sort of battery upon which the spell is fed. The stronger the power source, the stronger the spell.

I suppose that if the will is strong enough then it can act in a similar way. To enhance the basic makeup of a spell.

It is the structure of the spell which is particularly difficult to navigate. The varied threads and connectors powering one component and distributing that energy where it is required by the structure of the spell. I started to think of this as a sort of circuitry. Connecting various electrical tubes which adjust and alter the power to create the proper effect much like an amplifier, takes an electrical signal and converts it into sound.

As I pulled on these threads, I found I could also protect them from the waves of willpower, making it more difficult for the power to flow correctly. Each step took me closer to the ultimate goal which, was to find the power source and turn it off.

I had already decided to dissemble the child. Not because I had the power to do it, but because of the particularly brutal way he was attacking me and my friend. I will not say it was a conscious decision. In fact, I think I was being more instinctual than anything. But inside, deep inside, I knew it had to be done.

Even if the child was simply a tool of the father, he was too powerful. I was barely able to breath with the effort it took to keep him from destroying Janis and me.

For the record, Janis told me later that she resisted for quite a while, but the child was too strong. Her defenses were battered down eventually and no matter how complex or powerful the spell she tried, he defeated it. In the end, she turned toward me and began the organ bursting spell. Yes, it would have killed me. I even felt it as it began to build but I was close by then. It became a race between my effort and her spell.

I became aware, after I cut one of the threads, that the spell constructed for the duel had been dissipated. Knowing that the duelists were free gave me little solace, as I was so deeply focused on the task at hand.

Janis was an expert caster and had used that spell on more than one occasion in the line of duty, but as luck would have it, she had run out of prepared spells and had to do all the preliminaries as well. This gave me the precious few seconds I needed to snip away the last strands of construct from Millen's power.

Magical power works both ways. It is the source and the effect of casting spells. Without connection to the greater world, it cannot be used and thus begins to whither.

Millen had an immense natural power reserve. The spark of magic in him would last for some time, but eventually it would die. That last strand cut him off from the thing he needed the most. The thing to which he was addicted. He could feel it slowly dying inside but could never structure it into a force of will or a spell again.

I suppose I should have felt sorry for him. In a way, he was worse off than I had been before I knew what I could do. He couldn't even feel the magic in the world around him. Just that ever decreasing, once supreme, part of himself.

As a cop, the job always seems to get harder. It isn't something everyone can do, and I hope my kids never end up in the business. I doubt they will. They hardly ever see me anymore. I'm more in the nighttime than the daytime, as the metaphor goes. And even though, I try hard to make them know how much I love them.

Then there is my wife. She has supported me all this time never realizing how much sacrifice she has made to have a life with me. I don't think I will tell her about the whole dissembler thing. It wouldn't seem right. I just hope I don't do anything to screw up our life together.

As far as the case goes, we'd cracked it alright. And it was due to the efforts of quite a few people. Oh, Janis and I did some of the heavy lifting, but the rest of the team was serious value added.

The child Millen had come to consciousness before birth and tasted his power while still in the womb. I doubt anyone will know how or why he killed his mother at birth. My guess would be he wanted out and she was in the way.

He'd been particularly talented at mental control even before he understood how to structure a spell. His father admitted later that he wanted to kill him when he was born, but the power of the child compelled him to protect and instruct him.

Over time, the highly structured casting method of the father was adopted by the child, and he was able to exert even more control over those around him. The social exercises meant to give the child a feeling of connection to others, had only reinforced his opinion of his own superiority. With no one to control him and nothing to stop him but his own adolescence, he began to extend his sphere of power in small but significant ways.

Then the gatherers started showing up. First, when he was only six or seven, then more and more often. He generally sent them off with minor mental blocks and controls placed on them, but soon more powerful gatherers came seeking his apprenticeship.

One particularly, from the Aresinia guild, made him think he might be in danger if they discovered his true power.

It was then he decided to use the duels as a way of ridding himself of the gatherers. I must say that there is a level of adolescent inexperience here that could be explored by psychologists should they wish.

The fact that this somewhat romantic way of disposing of the threat was his choice could be traced, I think to his immature mind. He still, even with all his power, did not understand that there might be consequences. To him, it was just a very elaborate, fantastical way of dealing with a problem.

I went back to work the next day. Nothing happened. Janis and I filled out our reports and did whatever we could to pass the day, which I might say was one of the few where we didn't have some case to work. Just after lunch we were called into the captain's office where we were greeted by more than a dozen members of the guilds.

To put the entire conversation in a nutshell, I was promoted to a new position in the force. The guilds seemed to be afraid of me and were almost repentant about some unknown offense. I realize now that it was not me particularly that scared them, but the idea that they now had someone who could render the ultimate judgement upon them should they step over the line.

The promotion was to detective adjudicator. This was a combination of the older titles for dissemblers and the modern practice of criminal detection I know. Still, it seemed important, and I felt as though I was vindicated and even elevated in the eyes of my peers. All my life I'd grown up thinking I was less than I should have been. The new knowledge about myself gave me a sense of purpose and importance.

I wondered if I would use my ability well.

I found the kids in the underground not far from the place where I'd interviewed them only a short time before. The cash I handed to each was probably more than they'd ever seen. I'd worked out a deal with the Magista to add some cash and send gathers to the tunnels to find these kids. Janis wanted to be there for Bill the older kid who was obviously the leader.

As they counted the money and offered furtive glances around to make sure no one was waiting to take it from them, Janis drew Bill aside and spoke to him in hushed tones.

I was unable to hear anything that was said but after a short interview he nodded. She strode over top me with Bill at her side.

“He is going to test for the Chavezan guild. I am offering to coach him so you should expect to see him in the office most days for the next few months,” She informed me.

“I’ll look forward to it,” I smiled.

Bill seemed both embarrassed and he also acted as though he were torn between spending time with the other kids and finally having a direction.

“Bill,” I said quickly. “You know what this place needs?” I didn’t wait for him to even consider a response. “A cop actually watching out for these people. I think you could do some real good here.”

He smiled and looked over at his young companions.

Janis, Bill, and I headed back to the office to begin his formal preparations. As we walked, he spoke about his newfound dreams of changing things for the underground as though it had been his dream all along.

Who is to say that it hadn't been. Who knows what dreams a person has. I guess the best thing we can do is try to make the good dreams of all the children come true.

As I thought that rather magnanimous thought I realized Bill had not really been a child for quite some time. Like all those who deal with too much in their youth, he had grown up fast and skipped ahead to be an adult.

"Maybe we should stop on the way and get some ice cream?" I offered.

The smile told me he still had a little bit of childhood left to live.

www.ingramcontent.com/pod-product-compliance
Lightning Source LLC
LaVergne TN
LVHW012052160826
845678LV00014B/2792

* 9 7 9 8 8 4 6 5 8 0 5 8 9 *